"It's over. Everything between you and me is over."

"Love is over, but love isn't the only emotion, or even the most enjoyable. It will be over when I say so. Not before."

"You've turned into a monster," she breathed.

"Maybe I have. And maybe you know why. Remember you owe me a debt, and while it's outstanding you belong to me."

Driven beyond endurance, she seized the diamond necklace and hurled it at him. "Take it!" she screamed. "I want nothing from you."

He caught it and tossed it aside like cheap glass. "This isn't the debt I meant," he grated. "You can return jewels, but how will you ever restore the other things you stole from me. My child...my heart...my life..."

Lucy Gordon cut her writing teeth on magazine journalism, interviewing many of the world's most interesting men, including Warren Beatty, Richard Chamberlain, Roger Moore, Sir Alec Guinness and Sir John Gielgud. She has also camped out with lions in Africa, and had many other unusual experiences, which have often provided the background for her books.

She is married to a Venetian, whom she met while on holiday in Venice. They got engaged within two days, and have now been married for over twenty-five years. They live in England in the Midlands, with their two dogs.

Two of her books, His Brother's Child and Song of the Lorelei, have won the Romance Writers of America RITA Award in the Best Traditional Romance category.

Books by Lucy Gordon

HARLEQUIN ROMANCE®
3515—THE DIAMOND DAD
3529—BE MY GIRL!
3548—BEAUTY AND THE BOSS
3561—FARELLI'S WIFE

Rico's Secret Child
Lucy Gordon

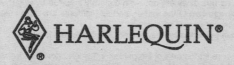

TORONTO • NEW YORK • LONDON
AMSTERDAM • PARIS • SYDNEY • HAMBURG
STOCKHOLM • ATHENS • TOKYO • MILAN • MADRID
PRAGUE • WARSAW • BUDAPEST • AUCKLAND

ISBN 0-373-03596-9

RICO'S SECRET CHILD

First North American Publication 2000.

Copyright © 1999 by Lucy Gordon.

Visit us at www.romance.net

Printed In U.S.A.

CHAPTER ONE

SHE'D longed to come to Italy, but not like this.

As Julie Hallam left the airport and got into the taxi that would take her to the centre of Rome, she suddenly knew that she'd made a terrible mistake.

On the face of it, she was to be envied—sophisticated, successful, arriving in the Eternal City with eight pieces of matching pigskin luggage filled with glamorous costumes and jewellery. Her clothes were expensive, her perfume musky, her grooming immaculate. She was a woman who'd made her way in the world and travelled to Rome on her own terms.

But long ago, she'd dreamed of coming here as the bride of Rico Forza.

She tried to put that thought out of her head. She'd survived the years since their parting by refusing to look back, but now it was as though all the memories she'd repressed had beaten down the doors at last, reminding her that here was something he'd described, and there was a place he'd promised to take her. And she would see them, but not with him.

'You are on vacation, *signorina*?' the taxi-driver called cheerfully over his shoulder.

'No, I'm here to work,' Julie called back, automatically putting on her bright, 'professional' face. 'I'm a nightclub singer. I have an engagement at La Dolce Notte.'

He gave a whistle of appreciation at the name of

5

Rome's most glamorous night spot. 'Then you must be very famous.'

'Not really,' she said, laughing.

'But La Dolce Notte hires only the best.'

'You've been there?'

'Not as a guest. One meal there would cost my earnings for a week. But many times I collect people in the early hours. Have you been to Rome before?'

'No,' she said quietly. She could have added, 'Only in my dreams.'

And what was a dream? Something that faded to nothing in the cold light of day and made you wish you'd never slept. In dreams, Rico took her in his arms, whispering, 'You're mine, *amore*, and nobody will ever part us.' But she always awoke to a cold, lonely bed and the knowledge that she would never see him again.

'Usually they employ only Italian singers,' the driver went on chattily.

She didn't want to talk, but anything was better than dwelling on her thoughts, so she said, 'I was singing in a London nightclub and this man was there at the front table. Afterwards, he came round and offered me this engagement. My agent said it was a big compliment. It's more money than I've ever earned before.'

The driver whistled respectfully. 'They must have been very anxious to secure you.'

It had seemed that way to her, too, and that puzzled her. Julie Hallam was a success and much in demand all over England, but she knew she hadn't reached the heights where foreign venues competed for her services.

Yet here she was, on her way to star at one of Rome's top nightspots. La Dolce Notte meant Sweet

Nights, and the club had a reputation for delightful decadence, liberally laced with money. Film stars and government ministers, the beautiful, the famous, the notorious, rubbed shoulders at its tables.

The manager had been so anxious to secure Julie's services that he'd provided free accommodation. It was close to the club, which would be useful for late hours.

The taxi had reached the Via Veneto, a broad, tree-lined avenue, full of expensive shops and open-air cafés. Halfway along, they turned into a side-road, stopping outside a large, ornate apartment block. The driver carried her bags inside, accepted her tip with a smile and departed.

The porter conducted her to an apartment on the second floor. 'Will you please call the club and inform them that you have arrived?' he requested with a small bow.

When she was alone, she looked about her in awe. She had a large living-room and a bedroom, both furnished in a palatial style. The huge bed was luxurious, as was everything else, including the bathroom. But the luxury made her uncomfortable. She was in Rome for three months, and it would have been nice to rent a cosy little flat. This place was more suited to an expensive kept woman.

She called the club and was put through to the manager's secretary. 'I'm afraid Signor Vanetti is out,' the woman said, 'but he would like you to be at the club tonight as his guest, and to meet some members of the press. A car will call for you at nine-thirty.'

Julie unpacked, then stripped off and showered, trying to dispel the unease that her surroundings had induced. She didn't belong in this opulent place.

Beneath the sophisticated façade, she still had much in common with the gauche girl who'd fallen in love with Rico Forza eight years ago. That girl had been called Patsy Brown, and her ambition was to be a singer. She'd taken a job at The Crown, a London pub, serving customers, collecting glasses. But every evening there was the music spot when she stood up and sang, accompanied by a pianist. The piano needed tuning and it was all very rough and amateur, but she could dream about being a *chanteuse*.

Then Rico had come to work there, and she'd discovered that life held more than singing.

He was twenty-three, an Italian visiting England to improve his English. He already spoke the language stiffly, but working at The Crown, he soon eased up and learned slang.

He was popular with the other bar staff and the customers. His comical mistakes endeared him to everyone. So did his ready laughter and the message that flashed from his dark eyes. He was tall and slim but strongly built, with a handsome face and a wide, sensual mouth. All the girls flirted madly with him, and he flirted madly back.

The only one he didn't flirt with was Patsy. When he spoke to her, it was always gravely, and sometimes his eyes rested on her with a burning, silent message that made her feel self-conscious. She began to realize that he watched her when she sang, standing stock-still as if entranced. And gradually she forgot everyone but him.

She stood there, her mass of fair hair framing her face like a halo, and sang the songs of youth and first love, of hopes and dreams that lasted for ever. And Rico never took his gaze from her.

Other men watched her, too, with slack mouths and drunken eyes, and one night, one of them was waiting as she left. His idea of a joke was to block her way, dancing about her in a way that made her feel sick.

'Please let me pass,' she begged in a shaking voice.

'All in good time. Why don't you stay and talk to me?' he said in a slurred voice.

'Because she doesn't want to,' said a voice from the darkness.

The lout whirled but wasn't in time to see the punch that connected with his chin. What happened then was too fast to follow, but suddenly her tormentor was running away, clutching his nose, and Rico was left there, blowing on his knuckles.

'Are you all right?' he asked gently.

'Yes, I—I'm fine.'

'You don't sound it. Come with me.' He drew her hand through his arm and walked for a few streets, saying nothing until they reached a fish and chip shop. 'Since I am in England, I am learning to like fish and chips,' he said. 'Cod? Plaice?'

'Cod, please,' she said.

'Sit down,' he commanded, pointing to a table for two by the window.

He brought plates of cod and chips, and large cups of tea, which he sugared liberally.

'I don't take sugar,' she protested faintly.

'You will take it now,' he said firmly. 'You've had a shock. You shouldn't be out alone at this hour. Why does your lover permit such a thing?'

'I don't have a lover,' she said shyly.

'That is an *infamia*. A beautiful girl should always have a lover. In my country, your solitude would be a reproach to every man.'

'And in my country,' she replied with spirit, ' a girl likes to be more than a trophy for the first man who can carry her off.'

'Not the first man,' he said softly. 'Only a man worthy of you.'

'And if I had a lover, I wouldn't ask his permission for anything I wanted to do.'

'If he was anything of a man, he wouldn't care whether you asked or not,' Rico retorted at once. 'If you were mine, I wouldn't let you walk alone in the dark.'

A silence fell between them. The conversation had opened up a minefield, and she wasn't sure she dared venture across. To cover her self-consciousness, she took a sip of tea. When she glanced up, she found him gazing at her with the look in his eyes that she'd seen before. But now it was more intense than ever, and something she found there made the colour flood her face, and her body burn as though a fire engulfed it.

'Why…are you looking at me like that?' she whispered.

'I'm thinking how much I want to make love to you,' he said simply.

She dropped her head so that he couldn't see her sudden shyness. No man had ever spoken to her with such frank intimacy before.

'You mustn't say that,' she said, blushing furiously.

'Why not?'

'Because—because we don't know each other. We've barely ever spoken before.'

'Words? What are they? I've watched you ever since the first day, and every time I've seen you, I've wanted to make love to you. I've thought how beautiful your lips are and what it would be like to kiss them.'

As soon as the words were said, she knew that there was nothing in the world she wanted as much as to kiss him. She was sure her desire must be obvious. She was completely vulnerable, with no defences against him. It alarmed her to realize that he could ask her anything and she couldn't refuse, wouldn't even want to try.

Before this, she'd been a well-organized person, her sights set on her ambition. Now everything was out of her control, and she was being rushed headlong to an unknown destination. She could run away, or she could put her hand into Rico's and let him lead her there.

She raised her head and gave him a glowing smile, full of trust.

He lived in a small backstreet boarding-house. They slipped in quietly and crept upstairs. He had one room that served as both bedroom and living-room, plus a kitchen no bigger than a cupboard, along with the use of a communal bathroom. Everything about it was shabby, but to her it was an enchanted place.

The bed was a bit cramped for two, but they didn't care. They had their passion and the beauty of its fulfilment.

She'd never made love with a man before, but with Rico everything seemed natural. He undressed her slowly, as though paying homage to her body, and when she was naked, his look of worship told her she was perfect.

'You are beautiful, *carissima*,' he murmured, his mouth against her smooth skin. 'Such beauty I've never seen before. I want to kiss you everywhere.'

He'd done just that, trailing his lips softly over her neck, her breasts, the inside of her thighs. Her shyness vanished under the sensations he was evoking. She had been made for this moment.

He loved her slowly, giving her time to overcome her shyness and relishing the beauty that she offered him as a perfect gift. Wherever his lips and hands touched her, he left a trail of delight.

'Rico,' she whispered, 'Rico—'

'Hush—trust me—say that you belong to me.'

'I belong to you,' she said, helpless against the rising tide of passion. 'Rico...Rico...oh, yes!'

She felt him seeking and claiming her. Nothing had ever felt so wonderful as the sensation of him inside her, loving her with passion and tenderness. She hadn't dreamed that there could be such joy.

His body was wonderful to her, young, strong and smooth, with the power to bring her own flesh to glorious fulfilment. She loved him for that, and for his gentleness. But most of all, she loved him because he was himself.

After their first loving, nothing was ever the same again. The world was bathed in new colours, each one bright and glowing. Now she knew what a man and a woman could be to each other, how passion could transform them into new selves and create another self that was neither one of them, but the love of them both together.

She moved in with him and found that he had many sides. There was the young man who'd arrogantly declared, 'If you were mine, I wouldn't let you walk alone in the dark.' But he could also be humble, treating her with reverence, passionately grateful for her love.

If he woke first, he would make tea and bring it to her in bed, watching anxiously until she'd sipped it and pronounced it perfect. Late at night, he would often cook for her, and when she protested that he did too much, he said simply, 'Nothing that I do for you is too much. You have given me everything.'

He said very little about his life in Italy beyond the fact that he came from Rome. She formed the impression that he'd grown up lonely and deprived of love. He was one of those rare men who knew how to appreciate what a woman had to give, not merely passion but affection. He loved her gentleness, her solicitude. When he started a feverish cold, she made him stay in bed and nursed him. He seemed overwhelmed by her care, as though nobody had ever looked after him before.

Then his mood would change and he would be merry, teaching her how to cook Italian food because, as he said, 'You're a disaster in the kitchen.'

Patsy had had nobody to teach her to cook since she was twelve and her mother had left home, unable to endure life with a husband who treated her as a slave.

The girl had been left to look after her father and brother, who expected to be waited on. Her father had been an idler, whose income came from cheating the social security system and the proceeds of petty crime, and he'd taught his son to do the same. She'd seldom had any money for herself because the two of them spent every penny in the pub.

She'd dreamed of escape, and her chance had come at seventeen when they'd both had to serve a short spell in prison. Patsy had slipped out of the house one night, made her way to the bus station and caught the next bus to London.

She'd told her story frankly to Rico. 'I'm going to make my own life,' she said fervently. 'I'll get engagements in the most glamorous places in the world and make lots of money and be my own woman.'

'Not mine?'

'Oh, Rico,' she said, instantly contrite, 'you know that's different. Of course I'm yours. It's just that…'

But there were no words to explain what drove her. With youthful confidence, she assumed that everything would work itself out, and she could have both her love and her career. For the moment, she simply enjoyed playing house, looking after her man, cherishing him in the little ways that seemed to mean so much to him.

'Who taught you to cook?' she asked one evening as he served her with spaghetti carbonara. 'Your mother?'

A strange look crossed his face. 'No,' he said after a moment. 'It was our—it was Nonna.'

'Your grandmother. That is—I believe that's what Nonna means.' She blushed in case he should suspect that she'd been studying Italian.

'Yes, it does. She wasn't actually my grandmother, but she was like one to me. When I was little, I used to spend time with her in the kitchen, telling her my troubles. She told me to make myself useful, so I chopped things and mixed things, and when I did it wrong, she yelled at me. And that's how I learned to cook.'

His manner was so droll that she laughed, then said, 'You told her your troubles? Not your mother?'

'Both my parents are dead,' he said, his humour fading. 'I'll get you some more tea.'

'No more, thank you. Tell me about your mother.'

'Another time.'

'Why not now? Darling, I want to know everything about you—'

'*Basta!*' he flashed. 'Enough!'

She stared. Rico had spoken softly but with an imperiousness that astounded her. For a moment, something flashed in his eyes that didn't fit with what she knew of him. How did a poor barman come to have that instinctive authority, that proud insistence on being obeyed?

Then, like lightning, he was his old self again, laughing, kissing her, making silly jokes. It might never have happened.

But that night, as she lay in his arms, feeling his body's warmth and the soft thunder of his heart close to her ear, the moment came back to her. Of course, Rico was Italian, and no doubt a touch of arrogance was normal in Italian men. Thus she tried to reassure herself and silence the little tremor of apprehension that warned her something ominous had happened.

When she awoke, the apprehension was gone in the blinding light of her happiness. She'd thought she knew what love was, but that seemed long ago in her ignorant girlhood, before she'd experienced the searing delight of the beloved man urgently claiming her. There were feelings that couldn't be described, like the hot pleasure as he entered her, whispering, '*Mio amore...sempre...per eternità...*'

Her emotion went too deep for speech, but her heart echoed his words: My love, always, for eternity. She couldn't see the change in herself or hear the new, deeper inflections in her voice, full of the memories of giving and taking, feeling his smooth brown skin next to hers, drinking in the intoxicating scent of male passion.

But these things were plain to everyone who heard her sing the songs of love. Her sensual awakening infused every word, every inflection, making her audience stop and listen with new attention and a sudden ache in their hearts.

Rico was a jealous lover, watching her with brooding eyes when she performed, angry with other men who saw her, although he knew she sang only for him. There was one song that she directed at Rico with special meaning.

Whatever happened to my heart?
I tried to keep it safe,
But you broke through
And stole it right away.
Take good care of it,
I'll never have another heart to give.

Once as they lay together, his head resting between her breasts, he whispered, 'You'll never leave me, will you, *carissima*?'

'Never,' she murmured.

'You must promise me,' he persisted urgently. 'Let me hear you say that you'll never leave me as long as you live.'

'I'll never leave you as long as I live,' she repeated, glorying in the words.

'And you'll never love another man.'

'I'll never love another man. Oh, Rico, how could I love anyone but you? You're all the world to me.'

She kissed him fiercely, and he responded with an abandon in which she thought she could detect a hint of desperation. As though he were afraid of something...

She didn't think of that at the time. Lying in his arms, her young body sated, she thought simply of pleasure. It was only later, when the world had collapsed and they were far apart, that she understood the strange note in his voice.

They'd had each other and the bliss of love fulfilled. And it had been enough, until the day they'd learned that someone else was about to enter their lives.

'A baby!' Rico had shouted with delight. He was an Italian. He'd been born with a father's heart. 'Our own baby. Our little *bambino*.'

He'd rushed out and bought her a locket with a picture of the Madonna and child. It was a cheap item, but to her it was pure gold, and she treasured it with her whole heart, especially when he took a coloured pencil to the Madonna's face and, with a few strokes, made it more like her own.

She'd been thrilled at his enthusiasm and the way his heart expanded at once to welcome their child. But her practical side wouldn't be silenced.

'Darling, we've no room for a baby and no money.'

'These things will sort themselves out. What matters is that we have a child of our own. And we will love it, and love each other, and love all the world because we are so happy.'

Had any young man ever been so recklessly full of joy? Where had it all gone?

With dreadful timing, her career had flared into life at that moment. The owner of The Ladybird, a small but elegant club, offered her an engagement. But Rico had insisted that she refuse it, which led to their first quarrel. He'd accused her of resenting their baby because it interfered with her career.

It wasn't true. She wanted his baby desperately, but she also wanted to be a star. And she was still young enough to think she could have it all. She'd learned better.

They'd made up the quarrel in each other's arms, and for a while all had been well. But the first crack had appeared.

Julie came out of her unhappy reverie to realize that she was staring into space. So much happiness crammed into such a short time. So much grief to follow. So empty the years since.

She gave herself a little shake. This was her moment of triumph, and she was going to give it all she'd got. And that meant refusing to think about Rico Forza or what might have been.

She slept for a couple of hours and rose in good time to get ready. Tonight she would be professionally 'on display', so she chose an elegant dark blue dress that shimmered as she moved and swept up her honey-blonde hair into an elaborate confection on top of her head. Her make-up was applied with great skill to look glamorous but discreet. It helped her feel she was banishing little Patsy who'd loved and lost, while conjuring up Julie Hallam, *chanteuse*.

At nine o'clock, she answered a knock on her door. A bellboy offered her a small package and vanished. She opened it, then stopped dead.

Inside was the most magnificent set of diamonds she had ever seen. Necklace, earrings, bracelet, even an ornament for her hair—all were flawless and obviously real.

The card said only, 'With the compliments of La Dolce Notte.'

Slowly she put them on, feeling more puzzled and uneasy by the moment. The diamonds must be worth thousands of pounds. Surely they couldn't be a gift?

But of course, they were only for display, and she would return them at the end of the evening. That must be it.

Precisely at nine-thirty, the receptionist rang to say that her car was ready, and she swept out to the luxurious limousine. The chauffeur held open the rear door. A man was sitting in the back, but all she could see clearly was the hand that he stretched out to assist her. She took it and felt him draw her inside. The door was closed behind them, the chauffeur got behind the wheel, and they were away.

Julie turned to look at the man sitting beside her. And she froze.

'*Buon giorno, signorina,*' said Rico Forza.

CHAPTER TWO

'RICO,' she whispered.

She felt as though her heart had stopped from the shock. Then she pulled herself together. She'd been thinking of him so much that she'd started imagining things. It was dark in the car except for passing flashes of light, and she peered, trying to see the man better.

'I'm sorry,' she said. 'I thought for a moment…'

A sharp beam of light swung round the car and away again. For a split second, it fell on Rico, his face a mask of cold, jeering triumph. Then it was gone.

His voice spoke from the semi-darkness. 'It was kind of you to wear the diamonds I sent you. Their splendour is matched only by your own.'

He didn't know her. But how could he? Eight years had so changed her that she hardly knew herself. Patsy Brown was dead and buried under a mountain of grief. Long live Julie Hallam!

'I am Rico Forza, the owner of La Dolce Notte, also of the hotel where you're staying,' he said smoothly.

I—I was expecting Signor Vanetti, the manager,' she stammered.

'And you find me instead. I hope you're not too disappointed. And your accommodation? Do you like it?'

She fought for something to say. At last she managed, 'Well…no, I would've preferred something smaller, less expensive. All that luxury oppresses me.'

'Excellent,' he said. 'The star who remains a simple

girl at heart. It's a good line. You should use it when you talk to the press tonight.'

'Must I?' she asked desperately. 'Of course I'll meet them, but perhaps not tonight.'

'I've already arranged it.'

The blunt assertion of power silenced her. Frantically she cast around in her mind for a way to end this. She must tell him the truth, but there was no time now. The short ride to La Dolce Notte was almost over. When they drew up to the kerb, he stepped out and reached in to help her. The hand that had once touched her with such reverent intimacy now held hers in a steely, indifferent grip. He wasn't even looking at her.

She drew on all her courage. This was going to be a difficult evening, but it would have been worse if he'd recognized her. Somehow she would find the strength to get through the hours ahead.

The outside of the club bore posters advertising the forthcoming appearance of 'Julie Hallam, glamorous singing star'. Two life-size pictures of her framed the door, and a small crowd on the pavement applauded when she appeared. Rico held out his arm, she slipped her hand through it, lifted her chin, and together they walked through the door.

There was more applause inside. Many of the staff were there as well as some photographers. Julie smiled into the flash bulbs and carried her head high.

The tables were arranged around a dance floor, where one or two couples were dancing smoochily to a small, expert band. Rico handed her to a table at the front with the ease of a practised host, then indicated for her to take her seat.

Now she could see him better. It was Rico and yet

not Rico. He was as handsome as ever, in fact more so. The unformed boy had grown into a man whose lines were clear and firm. Something in his face that might have gone either way had settled for hardness. His dark eyes, whose depths had once held such tenderness, now seemed to swallow light and reflect back only some cold, alarming emotion.

Since she'd found him in the car, she'd felt numb with shock. Now her heart had returned to life and was thumping uncomfortably. Their last meeting had been when he left for Italy 'to tell my family about you, about our love, and our baby'.

The parting was to be a matter of only a few days, but they'd never seen each other again.

'Why can't I come with you?' she'd begged.

'Because...it's best this way.' Rico had spoken uneasily, and soon, in misery and despair, she'd found out why.

And what of his despair, when he'd returned to find her vanished, leaving behind a letter that would break his heart and the locket he'd given her with such love? Since then, she'd wept many tears for his pain, wondering what that betrayal would do to him. Looking at him now, she thought she knew.

She remembered his open-hearted relish for life and people, his desire to give more than he took. But something had drained all that from his face, leaving behind reserve, caution, mistrust. This handsome, wealthy man with the world at his feet had a withered heart.

And it was her fault. If only her courage hadn't failed her all those years ago...

On the table lay a small packet, elegantly wrapped in gold paper.

'Open it,' he said. 'It's yours.'

'But—but there's no need. I mean…these…' She touched the diamonds about her throat.

'Open it,' Rico repeated in a quiet, dead voice.

Inside was an emerald bracelet. He fastened it onto the same wrist where she'd placed the diamonds. Her hand felt strange and top-heavy.

'It's lovely, but it's not necessary for you to shower me with jewels,' she protested. She touched the necklace again. 'Of course, I understand that these aren't mine. You wish me to wear them for tonight, but they belong to the club.'

'Have I said so?' he asked with a shrug.

'No, but you can't really mean to give a fortune in jewels to a woman you don't know.'

'It's strange, but I have the feeling that I do know you. Why would that be, *signorina*?'

'I don't know,' she said softly.

'The jewels are yours, all of them. Such a beautiful woman should attract expensive tributes from men.'

The emphasis on 'expensive' was faint but unmistakable, and his ironic tone almost turned the words into an insult. Julie began to feel as if she were moving through a nightmare. For years, she'd imagined that she might meet Rico again. In dreams, she'd run into his open arms. He would hold her close, telling her how much he'd missed her, but at last they were together again for ever.

Instead, she found a bleak-eyed stranger, who radiated hostility even while he played the perfect host. There was no tenderness in his voice, only a kind of grating quality that made her uneasy.

His shoulders were broader than she recalled, and his whole frame seemed heavier. He was still lean, without an ounce of fat, but the slender lad had been replaced by a man whose every line proclaimed power, force, dominance. He was a man to fear.

'Champagne,' Rico said to the waiter.

They'd drunk champagne together once, a cheap half bottle bought at cost price from the pub. They'd sipped from tooth glasses, giggling like children, and it had been delicious. The champagne he offered her now was like liquid gold, three hundred pounds a bottle, chilled to perfection. She could barely get it down.

'I've taken the liberty of ordering for you,' Rico said. 'Lobster salad, followed by…'

Bread and cheese, spiced up with the remains of a jar of pickles, washed down with lemonade. And love.

'The press will be visiting our table,' he said. 'Your arrival has caused great interest.'

'I didn't know anyone over here had heard of me.'

'I have ensured that they do.'

'Why are you here with me tonight? Surely it's the manager's job?'

'True, but I like to involve myself with this club. I have many investments, but some give me more pleasure than others. It suited me to be your host tonight.'

Something in his tone made her say, 'And you always do what suits you?'

'I do now. It wasn't always possible, but I've taken steps to ensure that these days things happen according to my wishes.'

'And other people?'

'I persuade them to see things my way.'

I will do anything, make any sacrifice for you, heart of my heart. Nothing matters to me more than to make you happy.

Had those words really been spoken by this same man?

No, another one, younger and full of hope. Something caught in her throat with pity for him.

Ironically it was the kind of night she'd dreamed of long ago. The food and wine were of the best; her diamonds sparkled under the lights. The press crowded around, but respectfully, with apprehensive glances at Rico. They, too, were afraid of him, Julie realized.

They began by addressing her in hesitant English but applauded when she responded in Italian. She described the highlights of her career, her favourite songs. 'I've also developed a repertoire of Italian songs, in honour of my Italian audience.'

They murmured approval, and a man asked, 'Have you ever lived in Italy, *signorina*?'

'No, never.'

'You have Italian relatives, friends?'

'Neither.'

'I was only wondering how you come to speak such good Italian.'

'I...' Briefly she floundered, then her quick wits came to her rescue. 'I've always wanted to visit this beautiful country and I prepared myself.'

The dangerous moment passed. Someone else said, 'Tell us about yourself. You have a husband, children?'

She could feel Rico's eyes burning into her as she answered in a stifled voice, 'No—neither.'

The questions lasted for a few more minutes until Rico brought them to an end by saying decisively, 'La Dolce Notte values its stars. It gives me great pleasure to present Signorina Hallam with this gift, one that I know she will value as no other woman could.'

He slipped a small box across the table towards her. Like the other one, it was wrapped in gold paper, and she had a sense of ill omen. Too many gifts and none of them given with kindness. There was something monstrously wrong here.

'Open it,' Rico said with a smile like a knife.

Although it was hard, she returned the smile and opened the little packet. And when she saw the contents, she drew a sharp, horrified breath.

It was a gold locket, studded with diamonds and sapphires. Inside was a picture of a Madonna and child, the very same picture that he'd given her long ago. She could still see the marks where he'd altered the face to make it like hers.

She looked up sharply and saw Rico watching her with eyes like stones. He knew her. Of course he did. He'd known from the beginning.

She had an eerie sense of pieces fitting together. It was unbelievable, and yet somehow inevitable. The club's determination to hire her was now explained. Rico Forza had bided his time for eight years until finally he'd lured her into his power.

He offered her his hand. 'We dance.' It wasn't a request.

She put her hand into his and felt him draw her to her feet and onto the dance floor. The band was playing a waltz, and his hand in the small of her back pulled her close to him, holding her firmly.

'Look at me,' he said quietly.

Glancing up, she found his mouth close to hers. How often had she kissed it? How hard and unforgiving it looked now!

'Rico,' she whispered.

'Smile when you say my name. People are watching.'

Calling on all her strength, she forced herself to smile, but she felt giddy. 'You knew me from the first moment, didn't you?'

'From before then, *signorina*.'

'Don't call me that.'

'It's a respectful way for a man to address a woman who is a stranger.'

'A stranger? Me?'

'You always were. There was a time when I thought I knew you—' he drew a sharp breath '—but I was wrong.'

'Don't hold me so close.'

'That's not what you used to say. You whispered, "Closer, Rico, closer. Make me a part of yourself."'

She didn't need the words to remind her. She could feel his body fitting against hers, the movement of his legs, recalling the steely power of his thighs and hips, power that had once made her cry out with pleasure. *Make me a part of yourself.* And he'd done so, again and again, until they'd been one person, for ever.

No, not for ever.

His mouth was so near to hers that she could feel his breath. 'You've forgotten all that, haven't you?'

'No,' she murmured, 'I'll never forget.'

'Then you decided to throw it away, and that's worse than forgetting.'

'It wasn't like that. There's so much to explain—'

'There's nothing to explain. It was all very clear.'

'And you think the worst of me, but you're wrong, truly you are. I want to tell you everything, but not here. Let me go...for pity's sake, let me go.'

The strain of being held against him was becoming

too much for her. In another moment, she would faint. Luckily the music was coming to an end.

'The cabaret's about to start,' Rico said. 'We'll leave now.'

Their departure was as much a triumphant ceremony as their arrival had been. She didn't know how she endured the short journey back to the hotel. As soon as they reached her suite, she turned to face him.

'Why?' she demanded passionately. 'Why?'

'Why what?' He was leaning against the door regarding her satirically.

'Why did you pretend not to know me?'

'Because it suited me to choose my moment. I've waited a long time. I could afford to wait a little longer. Let me look at you.' She tried to back away, but he gripped her shoulders and held her still while his eyes raked her. 'You look very different from what I remember, but then, my vision of you was always a delusion, wasn't it?'

'No, never. I loved you. That's the truth.'

He gave a mirthless laugh and released her suddenly. 'You used to be a better liar than that. Perhaps too much practise has blunted your edge for the finer subtleties of deception.'

'It was no deception,' she cried wildly. 'I loved you, Rico.'

'You loved me. You loved me so much that you deserted me while I was away preparing my family. I can still see myself returning home, running up the stairs, calling your name, waiting for the moment when you would throw open the door and enfold me in your arms.

'But you weren't there. There was only emptiness—

and your letter to me.' He took a step closer and said softly, 'Shall I remind you what that letter said?'

'No!'

'It burned itself into my brain so cruelly that even now I could repeat it word for word.'

'Don't,' she pleaded desperately.

'"We had a good time together, but nothing lasts,"' he recited. '"I've been thinking while you were away and I know what I really want from life." Do you remember writing that?'

'Yes,' she choked.

'You astonish me. Why should something so trivial linger in your mind? And the locket I gave you, that I chose with such love, to honour you as the mother of my child? Tossed aside as nothing.'

'And you gave it back to me tonight on purpose,' she accused.

'Covered in diamonds, a currency I thought you'd appreciate. You didn't want what a poor man could offer you. You wanted money, success and admirers. I shouldn't have taken my eyes off you for a moment, but like a fool I trusted your love. And then you were gone. So was my child. But I don't have to ask what happened to my child, do I? You never really wanted a baby.'

'That's not true,' she cried.

'Don't lie to me. I have a long memory. I can remember what you said about the problems babies brought, money, space—'

'I was just trying to be practical.'

'Oh, you were practical, all right. To me you were sacred. Our baby was sacred. But to you it was just an inconvenience. How foolish of me to expect you to interrupt your career to look after a baby.'

'You blame me for a great deal, Rico, but were you fair to me? You never told me you came from a great family who wouldn't think I was good enough for you. You left me to face your lawyer unprepared.'

'What the devil are you talking about?'

'While you were away, your grandfather's lawyer came and forced me to give you up.'

'I don't believe you. My grandfather was delighted at my news. He wanted me to settle down.'

'That may be what he said to you, but he was actually scheming to separate us. He sent a man called Vanzani to say that if I didn't leave you, he'd arrange to have you locked up. I couldn't take the risk.'

'I've never heard of the name Vanzani. The family lawyer is called Piccere.'

'I only know what he told me. He forced me to write to you—'

'Did he force you to return my locket as well?' Rico demanded in a voice that was almost a sneer.

'Yes, he did.'

'Oh, please, you can do better than that. If any of this were true, you could have contacted me. I'd have protected you from anyone.'

'It wasn't me they were threatening. It was you. I did it for you.'

'That's very good,' he said sardonically. 'If I still had a heart, I'm sure it would be melted by such a line. As I haven't, I advise you not to waste your time.'

'No,' she said slowly, looking at him. 'You have no heart now, have you?'

'Not since you destroyed it. I should be grateful to you. Life is so much more convenient without a heart. There's no pain. I once felt things far too much…' He checked himself with a sharp breath. 'Well, you know about that.'

'Yes, I used to be afraid for you because you felt everything so much,' she said. 'It meant you were always in danger. I wanted to stand between you and the world's pain, but...I couldn't. I didn't want to leave you, but I had no choice. It's the truth, Rico. Please believe it.'

He regarded her, his mouth twisted in cruel irony. 'Believe you? I'm not that much of a fool any more. The discovery that the woman I loved had betrayed me sent me a little crazy. Perhaps I still am. Be very careful what lies you tell me now. I'm a dangerous man to cross.'

'Yes, I can see how different you are,' she said slowly. 'The Rico that I loved would never have behaved as you have tonight. What do you want? Why have you loaded me down with all these jewels?'

'Call them the symbol of your success. Only I know the price you paid for that success. Tell me, *signorina*, was it worth it?'

She wanted to cry out that nothing had been worth the pain of losing him. If she could have found the words, she would have told him of the long, lonely years, aching for his love, knowing that no other man could be to her what he had been. But looking into the eyes of this cruel stranger, she knew that she could say none of this. He wouldn't understand.

The jewellery he'd loaded onto her seemed to burn her skin. She began to strip it off. 'Take it,' she said with horror. 'Take it all.'

'Don't tell me you no longer appreciate the luxuries of life,' he said ironically, 'especially when you've worked so hard for them?'

'You know nothing about me now, Rico. We're strangers to each other, and the sooner I'm gone the better. We should both try to forget that we ever met again.'

'What makes you think you're going to leave?'

'Do you think I'll stay now? I'm out of here on the next plane.'

'If you try that, I'll come after you and fetch you back. And I'll make sure the world knows how Julie Hallam treats her contracts. You'll never work again.'

The ruthlessness in his eyes shocked her. He meant every word.

'But can't you see how impossible this is,' she cried.

'You have a contract. You keep it. What's impossible about that?'

'For you and me—to work together—feeling like this.'

'Like what?'

'With all the past between us—'

'You're wrong,' he said harshly. 'I feel nothing where you're concerned. Nothing at all. Except perhaps anger at a woman who's trying to get out of her promises. But you'd know all about that, wouldn't you? After all, what is a promise? Something to be tossed aside when it suits you. You did that to me once. I won't allow you to do it again.'

'I think you must be a monster. All this time, you've sat planning your revenge like a spider at the centre of a web. How long have you been watching me?'

'Long enough. You weren't easy to find. Patsy Brown vanished very completely. But I went on searching because I had an old, unforgiven wrong to avenge. For the next three months, you belong to me.'

'I belonged to you once,' she said, hardly able to breathe. 'But not any more.'

'You belong to me now,' he said, taking her shoulders and forcing her to face him. 'I've paid your price in advance. I thought you would appreciate that.'

'My price? Are you daring to suggest that I—'

'Know how to drive a hard bargain. I respect that, but so must you.' His voice became soft, deadly. 'You've been bought and paid for. Knowing the kind of woman you are, I'm sure you understand.'

CHAPTER THREE

BOUGHT and paid for.

The words echoed in her head, the cruelest kind of insult, but one he felt she deserved. And as though a flash of lightning had illuminated the world, she saw herself through his eyes, a woman whom any man could insult because she'd traded her heart for gold.

As if to confirm it, he added, 'I've paid in the currency you understand. Diamonds, champagne, luxury. I always pay my bills in full.'

'I won't make that kind of bargain with you,' she gasped, outraged.

'You've already made it. And you'll keep it.'

'No,' she cried, trying to wrench herself away. But his fingers were iron on her shoulders, drawing her closer until she was pressed hard against him. Then his mouth was on hers in a swift movement that left her no chance to struggle.

She raised a hand to fend him off, but he had twice her strength. One arm went behind her neck, the other around her waist, holding her helpless while his mouth moved over hers with hard, driving purpose that angered her even while she felt her loins responding to it.

She knew now that from the moment she saw him tonight, she'd been waiting for this, wondering if his lips would feel as good against hers as they always had. But they weren't his. They belonged to a cruel stranger, and after the first shock of pleasure, her head cleared and everything in her denied him.

'I...won't...let you do this,' she said desperately.

'No blushing violet act, please. Surely those diamonds entitle me to something better?'

He covered her mouth again before she could answer, and this time his tongue found its way to its old home, where once it had been so welcome. Her responses to the flickering tip were still there, still waiting for him after all this time. Fire. Passion. Eager desire. Wanting him. Only him. Forgetting all else.

'No...'

The denial came up from deep within her, but it was words only. Her quivering flesh consented despite all her resolutions. She had a terrifying sense of danger, not from him but from herself. After all this time, his touch could send her wild, making her want him as much as before, while his own heart remained cold. For him this was an exercise of will, and if she yielded now, she would earn only his contempt. And her own.

'No! Rico, stop this, please—'

'I've paid for you,' he said grimly. 'And what I've paid for, I will take.'

Once he'd kissed like a boy with his first love. Now he kissed like a man who'd kissed too often and for the wrong reasons. But she, too, had changed. She'd become what she once told him she would be. Her own woman. Pride and self-respect revolted, and she fought him in the only way she could—with stillness. It was difficult because the fire was raging in her, but she called up all the strength she'd learned in the hard years.

At last, the message of her silence got through to him. He drew back and looked at her, his eyes glittering. 'How you've changed! Once you knew how to give. Now you know how to withhold, but no matter, since I've learned to take. The years have made you more beautiful, and taking will be a pleasure.'

She couldn't speak for the thundering of her heart. She could only watch his eyes with their strange look, as though they were seeking the very depths of her.

'Kiss me,' he said quietly.

'No,' she said. 'Not like this.'

'Kiss me,' he breathed against her mouth. 'Kiss me with lies on your lips, as you did before. But this time, I shall know that they're lies and then I'll be cured of my memories.'

'You can't cure memories, Rico. I've tried hard enough.'

'Do you think I'll be a prey to them all my life?' he raged. 'Kiss me now, so that I can watch you being the cynical little schemer you are.'

Her courage came flooding back. 'Are you sure that's all I am, Rico? Is it so hard to convince yourself?'

Without giving him the chance to answer, she did what he'd demanded and kissed him. Her lips were soft and they lingered on his, purposely conjuring up memories that went back beyond his bitterness, memories of the boy and girl they had been.

'Is that how you mean, Rico?' she whispered.

She wasn't fighting him now but melting in his arms, challenging him to go on hating her while she worked sweet magic on his senses. She caught a glimpse of his face, filled with desperation, felt his arms tighten about her, and the next moment she was lying on the bed with him beside her. Her heart filled with hope, but his words destroyed it.

'You're more skilful than I thought.'

'Wh-what?'

'You knew just what to do, didn't you? Nice to know we're two of a kind. Now we can just enjoy ourselves.'

His lips traced the line of her jaw, teasing her lightly as they moved over her skin, down her long neck to the base of her throat. If only his heart was in this, it would be wonderful, but he'd set out the terms. Barter and exchange—a cold, bitter bargain between two people who neither loved nor trusted each other.

Whatever he said about being strangers, as lovers they knew each other as well as any man and woman ever had. Rico knew the sensitive spot beneath her ear where she loved to be kissed, knew the little pulse that throbbed at the base of her throat when she was aroused. These memories still lived in him, and he made skilful, pitiless use of them.

'You devil...' she whispered.

'Not a devil,' he murmured back. 'Just a man who knows your body well, if not your heart. And your body is all I want. It remembers me, too, doesn't it?'

'Yes,' she gasped.

'I wonder how many men have kissed you over the years. Did they know you as I did? Did they understand the little signals you give to show a man that he's pleased you—or tell him what you want him to do? Or do you keep a different set of signals for every man?'

The contemptuous words were like a flood of freezing water, shrivelling her passion. Julie's eyes flashed with anger and she mustered all her force to thrust him off. 'Get out,' she cried. 'Get out of here now.'

She'd taken him by surprise. He gave a sharp intake

of breath, then his mouth twisted ironically. 'Perhaps you're right. Some things are better postponed. The anticipation is a pleasure in itself.'

'Never,' she choked. 'That will never happen.'

'Don't be so sure, *amore*.'

'Don't call me that. It's over. Everything between you and me is over.'

'You're wrong. Love is over, but love isn't the only emotion, or even the most enjoyable. It will be over when I say so. Not before.'

'You've turned into a monster,' she breathed.

'Maybe I have. And maybe you know why. Remember, you owe me a debt, and while it's outstanding, you belong to me.'

Driven beyond endurance, she seized the diamond necklace and hurled it at him. 'Take it!' she screamed. 'I want nothing from you.'

He caught it and tossed it aside like cheap glass. 'This isn't the debt I meant,' he grated. 'You can return jewels, but how will you ever restore the things you stole from me? My child...my heart...my life—'

He stopped abruptly and the silence seemed to echo with his anguish. His face was white and shocked, as though he'd revealed too much and despised himself for it.

'Rico,' she pleaded, 'it wasn't like that. If only I could make you understand—'

'For pity's sake, shut up! Do you think I care what you have to say? Will explaining change the past?'

'It might help you understand it.'

'And will understanding give me back my child?'

'Rico, I—about our baby...' It was on the tip of her tongue to tell him everything, but a thousand fears screamed in her mind.

'Yes?' he asked harshly.

'Nothing.'

He seemed to withdraw into himself. The fierce bitterness that had possessed him fell away, to be replaced by bleak formality. 'It's late. You should get some sleep to prepare for your first rehearsal tomorrow morning.'

'Don't worry. I'll be there.'

'Then I'll bid you good-night and offer you my best wishes for a successful engagement at La Dolce Notte.'

'Rico,' she whispered.

'Welcome to Rome, *signorina*.'

He gave her a small bow that was like a slap in the face. Then he was gone.

She stood staring at the door, unable to move. She didn't cry because she'd cried herself dry long ago. But she was possessed by pain such as she'd thought she would never know again.

How could he have accused her of such things? How could he believe that she would betray their love by giving away his child? The truth was so different. So very, very different.

She'd known that something was badly wrong when she opened the door and found the sharply dressed man standing there. He was terrifyingly neat and tidy, with short hair slicked into place, and she'd become awkwardly aware of her shabby dress.

'I'm looking for Signorina Brown.'

'I'm Patsy Brown.'

She stood back to let him pass. He gave the room the same appraising look that he'd given her. His smile was half a sneer.

'I dare say you've been expecting me, *signorina*.'

'No. Why should I? I don't know who you are.'

'My name is Ettore Vanzani. I am a lawyer and I represent the Forza family in this matter.'

'What matter?'

'The matter of your attempted entrapment of Rico Forza.'

'My what?' she asked, aghast. 'What are you talking about?'

'Please, *signorina*, no denials. We both know how things stand. You've played your cards very cleverly. Rico himself thinks you're pregnant—'

'It's true. I'm carrying Rico's child. I love him. We're going to be married—'

'Yes, yes, you have a very strong hand. The young man is besotted with you, and you can ask a high price from his family.'

'That's nonsense! Rico's family is as poor as I am.'

'His people, as you know, are wealthy bankers who would pay a good deal to free him from this entanglement.'

'Nonsense. If Rico comes from a rich family, why is he living like this?'

Vanzani shrugged. 'Youthful rebellion takes many forms. A young man who has had every luxury since birth probably finds these surroundings romantic.'

His cool assurance was frightening. It was impossible that what he was saying was true. And yet…

'I don't believe you,' she said weakly. But she was trying to silence the fears that shouted in her mind. 'Rico loves me. He went home to tell his family that we were to be married—'

'He certainly told them that. His grandfather immediately contacted my firm to have you investigated.

The Forza family is choosy about who marries into it. Your own family doesn't stand up to scrutiny. Your father and your brother are petty criminals, constantly in and out of prison.'

'That's not my fault.'

'In my country, family connections matter. Signor Forza will do anything to stop his grandson from marrying you. And I assure you, anything means anything.'

'Are you daring to threaten me, my baby—'

'The threat,' Vanzani said silkily, 'is rather to Rico himself. His grandfather will have him locked up, if necessary, until he comes to his senses.'

Suddenly courage came to her. 'I don't believe a word of it,' she said flatly.

'Then tell me this. If Rico is poor, why am I here? Who pays my fee? Who would care whom he married?' While she struggled to find an answer, Vanzani opened his briefcase and took out an envelope. 'You may find these of interest,' he said coolly.

The envelope contained photographs. The centre of each one was a young man, clearly recognizable as Rico when he was younger. This was Rico as she'd never seen him, dressed in expensive clothes, standing against backgrounds of palatial luxury. In one picture, he was mounted on a horse that looked like a thoroughbred. In another, he was with an old man with a hard, lined face.

'That is Arturo Forza, the head of the family and Rico's grandfather,' Vanzani said.

'Why did you bring these?' Julie asked, and to her own ears her voice sounded thin and unnatural, the voice of someone fighting off hysteria.

'In case you needed convincing.'

'But you said I'd always known about Rico's background. If that were true, why should I need convincing?'

Vanzani acknowledged a hit. 'You're intelligent, *signorina*. Very well, I acknowledge that I wasn't quite sure. Perhaps you're truly the innocent you claim. In that case, I pity you, but it makes no difference. The old man won't tolerate you in the family, and he'll smash Rico rather than let it happen.'

'But if he understood that I really love Rico, that I could make him happy...' The words withered and died under Vanzani's sneer. This man, and those who employed him, weren't concerned with feelings. She made one last try. 'You're bluffing. I don't care how powerful his grandfather is. People can't get away with that kind of behaviour these days.'

Vanzani didn't answer this in words. He merely pointed to the wicked old face in the picture. She believed him then. A man with such a face was capable of anything.

To her horror, she was suddenly swept with nausea. She clapped a hand to her mouth and fled the room, running along the corridor to the little bathroom. When she returned, she was white and shaking.

'I suppose your pregnancy is real,' Vanzani said with a shrug. 'That's a pity, but the marriage is still impossible. I'm not bluffing. My employer has friends in government and in the police. Rico can be arrested on trumped-up charges and held behind bars as long as necessary.'

It was fear for Rico that made the decision for her. Vanzani saw the moment of defeat in her face and went into action.

'My employer is not unreasonable,' he purred. 'I

have here a banker's draft for ten thousand pounds. This will compensate you for any distress. You will write to Rico breaking off your relationship and you will make no further attempt to contact him. If you disobey, the consequences will be dire—for him.'

He insisted on having the letter immediately. Feeling as though she were dying inside, she wrote it, but he pushed it back to her.

'That won't do. It has to be convincing. You should put in some little detail from the life you shared with him. Something about your singing career, perhaps.'

'How do you know about that?'

'Rico told his grandfather all about you. It was very touching. Get on with it.'

Somehow she managed to get the dreadful letter written.

'He'll see through it,' she whispered, choking with grief. 'When you give him this, he'll know you made me write it.'

'You're going to leave it here when you go. He'll find it when he returns. But he won't find you unless you want very bad things to happen to him. This place, and the pub where you work, will be watched and the mail checked. I'm warning you not to write and to stay well clear.'

He read the letter through and grunted. 'It'll do, but there should be something else.' His eyes raked her, taking in the locket about her neck which she'd instinctively clutched. 'Did he give you that?'

'No,' she said hastily. 'No, he didn't.'

'You're lying. Let me see.'

She tried to back away, but he seized the chain and yanked the locket from her neck with one ruthless jerk.

She screamed, but he shrugged and turned away, clicking the locket open.

'A Madonna and child,' he sneered. 'How touching.'

'Give it to me!' she screamed. 'Give it to me, *please*.'

'You have no further use for it. Get your things together now.'

But she couldn't move. This last cruel detail had sapped her courage, and she collapsed with her head on her arms, sobbing frantically. Vanzani hauled her to her feet and shook her.

'Shut up!' he snapped. 'This won't do you any good, do you hear? Do you hear?'

He shook her again, and it had the effect of clearing her head. This was a brutal man, and if she stood up to him, he might do something that would harm her child. She forced herself to calm down and nodded obediently.

'Good.' He released her. 'Now get your things. I won't tell you again.'

No detail was left to chance. He'd taken her to an hotel that night and kept her there for a week. Then, suddenly, it was over.

'Rico has returned and found your letter,' Vanzani told her. 'He spent some time searching for you, but now he has accepted your decision and returned home to Italy. You are free to go. Anywhere you like, except that room and the bar where you used to work.'

He had one final thing to say. 'Rico Forza must not be named as the father of your child. This can be checked. Do not disobey.'

She found a room to live, shut the door and cried without stopping for two days. She cried until there was nothing left inside her heart but emptiness. It was the thought of her baby that brought her back to life. She forced herself to eat and grow strong, but she tasted nothing.

Vanzani had vanished, but even so he seemed to control her. Briefly she thought of asking a mutual friend to call Rico, but they had none. They'd been everything to each other, with no need for anyone else. She dreamed of a thousand ways of contacting him but abandoned them all. The fear of causing Rico harm paralysed her.

At last, she left London, settled in a small midland town where nobody knew her and began wiping out all traces of her past identity. Her new name, Julie Hallam, was an invention that couldn't possibly be traced back to Patsy Brown.

She lived frugally, making the money last as long as possible. She would have loved to hurl it back at the cruel Forzas, but she needed it for her baby. She could never destroy her last link with her beloved.

Her little son had his father's dark eyes and hair, and she longed to name him Richard. But it was too much like Rico, and she was frightened even to venture that tiny step. In the end, she called him Gary. As he grew, she also found in him Rico's warmth and intensity, plus his mercurial nature. Sometimes he was so like his father that her heart ached, but he brought joy to her life and made everything worthwhile.

It was hard to pursue a career and raise a child, but a stroke of luck put her in touch with a distant cousin in her fifties. Aunt Cassie, as Julie and Gary called her, was lonely and only too glad to take them in as lodgers. If Julie had to be away, she cared for Gary like a second mother.

Gradually Julie Hallam worked her way up the billboards until she reached the top. The slight chubbiness that had blurred her features at seventeen fell away, leaving her face fine with hollows under the cheekbones. As her success increased, so did her elegance and sophistication. She could project a song with a subtle sensuality that made club managers clamour for her services.

It was the career she'd dreamed of, but now it came second to the precious moments when she could close the front door behind her, open her arms to her darling son and leave the world behind.

She raised him to speak Italian as well as English, learning it herself so that they could converse in his father's language.

Many times during those years, she thought of Rico with pity for the joy he couldn't share. Perhaps one day, she reflected, they would meet again, then she could show him his son and see the pride in his eyes.

But now the meeting had come, and it was a disaster. Rico had planned this for a reason. After eight years, he wanted his revenge.

She slept badly. Her dreams were filled with Rico as he had been long ago. His hands touching her gently, then with eager purpose, his voice murmuring, 'My love—for ever.' Then the feel of him inside her, filling her with pleasure and satisfaction, filling all the world with love. And the fierce, joyful heat of two melting into one.

Every image was one of warmth, and now she saw clearly how that warmth had infused their whole relationship night and day. His hands had been warm as had his heart. When he smiled at her, the warmth in his eyes had seemed to reach out and enfold her, protecting her from the world.

But the world had broken through. All their love hadn't been enough to save him from having his heart broken, and now everything in Rico seemed to have turned round to its opposite. Love had become hate, and joy had turned to bitter, icy vengeance. Once he'd treated her with reverence. Now he regarded her with contempt.

She looked back over the terrible scene between them, wondering why she hadn't told him that she'd kept his son with her, treasuring the child as her last link with the man she loved. But she'd been too frightened of him. He was a man without a heart. He'd boasted of it. A man who used authority and self-will to fill the void where feeling had once been.

And this dreadful change in Rico had been the work of years. It couldn't be reversed by one disclosure, however welcome. Now he cared only for *vendetta*, and what better revenge than to punish her by snatching her son?

And so he must never know that Gary lived with his mother. She must get through these next few weeks and then escape him, without letting him suspect her secret. It would be a test of endurance, but she had already proved herself a survivor.

CHAPTER FOUR

HER first rehearsal was next morning. She dressed for it plainly, in russet slacks and a fawn silk shirt, with the barest minimum of make-up. As she was about to leave, the phone rang, and a man's voice spoke from the desk downstairs.

'Your car is here, *signorina*.'

'I'm not expecting a car.'

'The club has sent one to collect you.'

She thanked him and went down to where Rico's driver was waiting. 'I'm sorry you've had a wasted journey,' she said, smiling at him. 'I prefer to walk.'

He paled. 'But the boss—'

'He'll understand.'

The driver's face showed that he doubted this, but Julie walked out of the hotel quickly. It was vital to her to keep these small signs of her independence.

But there was another reason. Yesterday she'd called home from the airport rather than waiting until she reached the hotel, for which she was now profoundly thankful. If she'd used the hotel phone, Rico would have a record of her home number.

All the negotiations for this engagement had gone through her agent, and it was clear that Rico didn't know where she lived or he would have known that Gary lived there, too. She must keep it that way.

She found a side-street and took out her mobile phone, thankful that she had one that could make calls abroad. In a few moments, she could hear her son's voice, feeling the little tremor of pleasure that it always gave her.

'Hallo, darling,' she said tenderly.

'Hallo, Mommy!'

'What were you doing when I called?' she asked as she always did.

'Aunt Cassie and me were washing up breakfast,' he said. He was still at the stage where washing-up was a game. 'But I broke a plate.'

She laughed fondly. 'Never mind, darling. I wouldn't care if you broke a hundred plates.'

He giggled, and a surge of happiness went through her. For him, anything was worth it.

They talked some more, and then he gave the phone to Aunt Cassie.

'Cassie, have you seen anybody hanging round the house?' Julie asked urgently. 'Any strange men, anyone come to the door?'

But she had seen nothing and nobody. Julie began to relax. But she wasn't taking chances.

'Remember when we went to the Lake District last year?' she said. 'I want you to go there again, today, this minute. Just put Gary in the car and drive. And don't tell anybody where you're going.'

'Julie, whatever's wrong?'

'I'll explain next time. But get Gary away today.'

'Can't we come over there and be with you?'

'No,' she said frantically. 'Please, Cassie, just do as I ask. Call me when you get there.'

She hurried the rest of the way to the nightclub and caused a sensation when she walked in off the street. The doorman, who'd seen her approach, was pale.

'The boss sent the car for you,' he muttered uneasily.

'I know. I simply preferred to walk.'

'But—' he looked nervously up and down the street
'—the boss said, well, he wanted you to take the car.'

She recognized the same frisson of fear that she'd
sensed in the driver. 'The boss' had to be obeyed. How
could this man be the Rico she'd known and loved?

But he was no longer that Rico. He was a different
man. She would be wise to remember that.

She hurried on into the club. A piano had been set
up on the stage, and a bald, middle-aged man was
seated at it, softly strumming. He rose and advanced
towards her with outstretched hands.

'I am Carlo Peroni, the musical director. I am so
pleased to see you.'

She liked him at once. There was a genial, no-
nonsense air about him that she knew she could work
with.

The club looked very different by day. The tables
were bare, the lighting harsh. The carefully constructed illusions of the night had been packed away
until needed. But Julie was content in this atmosphere.
This was where she worked, doing what she was good
at, preparing an act that would please her audience. It
was also how she managed to survive, by pushing
painful feelings aside and submerging herself in her
music.

They ran through a couple of songs while he listened closely to the timbre of her voice. Mildly he
suggested a couple of key changes. She tried them and
was pleased with the result. She began to relax. But
her peace was shattered by the sound of a door closing
sharply as someone entered the club.

Rico strode down the tiered rows of tables to stand
watching her at the front. He was angry.

'Good morning,' he said to her coldly.

He was casually dressed in white shirt and slacks and, despite the informality, was perfectly groomed. The shirt was crisp and snowy. Had she really once seen him living in jeans?

'I sent the car for you,' he snapped.

'I preferred to walk.'

'And I prefer that you follow my wishes.'

It took courage to stand up to the man he had become, but she forced herself to do it.

'Don't try to control my every movement, Rico,' she said softly. 'I'm here and I'll fulfil my engagement, but that's all. You don't own me.'

'I thought I'd made it plain that I do.'

'You think you do, but I won't let you. You're such a different person that I don't know you any more—'

'We'll discuss that sometime—'

'But I'm a different person, too. I'll stay here, but I'll fight you if I have to.'

His face became hard with anger. Then his mouth twisted, and he shrugged. 'Very well. War it is.'

He stepped back and swung out a chair, seating himself on it and leaning back with an expectant air.

'Are you going to stay here?' she asked in dismay.

'Why not? I've made a heavy investment in you. Naturally I want to study your progress. You object?'

It was useless to protest. She shrugged and returned to the piano, where Carlo was quietly fingering the keys. He gave Rico an abstracted greeting. He was one of the few people who weren't afraid of him, Julie came to realize.

They resumed. Carlo already knew most of her material, and they were soon working together easily, stopping here and there to try out a phrase in a new way. It would have been a good rehearsal but for her awareness of Rico, watching her, a prey to thoughts she could only imagine.

When they took a break, Julie found coffee waiting for her at Rico's table. She could stand it no longer. 'Please go,' she said as firmly as she could manage. 'You're distracting me from my work.'

'I'm sure that such an experienced professional isn't that easily distracted,' he said smoothly. 'Besides, I can't resist the chance to watch you exercise your charms again.'

'What I do on stage is an act,' she insisted. 'It has nothing to do with what I feel in my private life.'

'Nonsense. Who knows better than I do that your private life, too, is an act?'

'You really do hate me, don't you?' she said softly.

'I'm glad you understood.'

'But how long can hatred last, Rico?'

'Longer than love,' he murmured. 'Years longer.' He raised his voice so that Carlo could hear. 'I've asked Julie, as a favour to me, to sing a special English song called "Whatever Happened to My Heart?"'

'No,' she said quickly. 'Not that one. I—I don't know it any more, and Carlo won't have the music.'

'But he has,' Rico said. 'I arranged for a copy to be sent to him. He's been practising it, haven't you, Carlo?'

'Night and day,' the plump little man replied cheerfully. 'Ever since the boss said this was an important song for him.'

And the boss's word was law. Julie felt a frisson of unease at how carefully Rico had planned everything. And yet try as she might, she couldn't help a brief, aching pleasure that the song still had some significance for him.

Carlo struck the first chord, and she began to sing in a soft, husky voice.

'Whatever happened to my heart?'

She refused to look at Rico. She didn't want to see him now. She preferred to remember the other Rico, who'd watched her with such adoration long ago in another life.

'I tried to keep it safe,
But you broke through
And stole it right away.'

She'd been right not to want to sing this. The past was too close, too painful still. He'd stolen her heart, leaving her in a wilderness.

'Take good care of it,
I'll never have another heart to give.'

At the end, she could hardly manage to sing. Her voice thickened as memory overcame her, and she faltered to a halt. Her eyes were blurred with tears. She brushed them away and sought Rico. Surely he, too, had remembered and been moved?

He was leaning back, applauding her ironically. 'The tears are good,' he said. 'Keep them. It looks convincing.'

She stared at him in disbelief, feeling herself die a little inside.

She forced herself to keep on, trying not to let her

growing agitation affect her voice. Rico didn't inter-
vene again, but she was aware of his eyes, cold, vengeful, not leaving her for a moment.

'That's enough,' he said at last. 'It's time for lunch.'

'Of course,' Carlo said easily. 'We'll share a glass
of wine.'

'Not today,' Rico said. 'Julie will have lunch with
me.'

He wound her fingers in his as he spoke. It looked
like a gesture of romantic possessiveness. Only Julie
was aware of the power of his grip and the steely
determination within him.

He took her to his office, which was two floors up,
with a view overlooking the Via Veneto. It was spa-
cious and airy, with huge windows that flooded it with
light. There was a large desk on which stood a few
items, neatly arranged.

Everything was clean, sparse, austere. The sense of
emptiness was like a terrible echo sounding through
her. How untidy he had once been! In those days,
everything about him had overflowed: his clothes, his
books, his heart, his joyous love of life. Now everything was neatly buttoned down. And dead.

A table was laid for two. The cloth was snowy, the
crystal gleaming. There was a bottle of sparkling mineral water and one of white wine.

'I ordered a light lunch for you,' Rico said, gesturing. 'I remember how little you ate when you were
singing. Wine?'

'Just mineral water, please.' Julie sat and waited
while he poured the glittering liquid.

In the bright light from the windows, she could see
his face better. He looked very pale and drawn, as

though he'd had a bad night. She wondered if it had been as bad as her own.

'I thought you'd like to know that I've done some investigating,' he said. 'And I discovered that Vanzani exists. He calls himself a lawyer, but he's more of a small-time enforcer.

'But at least you know that I was telling you the truth,' she said eagerly.

'He remembers going to see you on my grandfather's orders,' Rico agreed.

'Well, then…'

There was no softening in his face. 'He also recalls something that you "forgot" to tell me—that you accepted a pay-off of ten thousand pounds.' He watched her face. 'Well? Aren't you going to deny it?'

'No, it's—it's true,' she stammered, 'but—'

'But what?'

'I was going to tell you about it,' she said truthfully, 'but last night everything was so confused…' She gave up in despair. Without telling him everything about Gary, there was no explanation she could make.

'No answer?' he mocked. 'Well, perhaps you're wise.'

'Yes,' she agreed. 'Too wise to waste my words on a man who's made up his mind in advance. Let it be, Rico. We have nothing more to say to each other.'

'Can you say that so easily?'

'Not easily. But let's face the truth. We've both changed beyond recognition. We can't go back to what might have been.'

'Tell me about my son.'

The abrupt demand, coming out of nowhere, made her stiffen. Rico's face was tense, unyielding, but revealed a terrible anxiety as he met her eyes.

'Tell me about my son,' he repeated softly. 'Or can't you tell me? Did you give him away without even seeing him?' His voice flicked like a lash.

'No, I—I saw him.'

'What was he like?'

'He was a big baby. He weighed eight pounds nine ounces. And he had lovely dark eyes.'

'I thought all babies had blue eyes for the first few weeks,' he said sharply.

'They were dark blue,' she amended quickly.

And they'd soon turned deep brown, matching his father's. But she couldn't tell him that.

'Did you ever hold him?'

In the first hour, she'd held him against her breast in a passion of love. She'd rained tears of joy and pain over the tiny form that lay in her arms, exhausted by his perilous journey. He'd been oblivious of the storms that raged about his head, while she wept and whispered, 'My love, my darling.'

Whom had she really been talking to?

'Yes, I held him,' she said.

'And then you gave him away,' Rico said bitterly. 'All these years he's lived with strangers, where I can't see him. My son. Mine!'

If she'd doubted her decision to keep Gary hidden, those doubts were silenced now. The look of brutal possessiveness on Rico's face as he said 'Mine!' confirmed her worst fears about the man he'd become. Arturo Forza had sent his emissary to crush her. And this was his heir.

'Tell me where he is,' Rico said harshly. 'Tell me where my son is. Tell me.'

'Forget him, Rico. You have no son.'

'Damn you!' he said softly.

'Do you think I'd want him growing up here, learning to be like you and him?'

'Him?'

'Your grandfather. A man who terrifies everyone into submission. I'll never let him near my child.'

'My grandfather died two years ago.'

'But he lived long enough to damage you, perhaps to make you like him. Don't forget, I've been on the receiving end of his ruthlessness. He threatened to have you locked up if I didn't give in. How could he do that if he loved you? But he didn't love you, did he? His own grandson!'

He looked uneasy. She'd got through to him.

'My grandfather loved people in his own way,' he said at last. 'That doesn't mean his feelings weren't real.'

'But his feelings were more pride than affection, weren't they?' she insisted.

'What do you think you know about him?' Rico demanded with swift anger.

'After the way he treated me, I know a great deal. "Loved people in his own way" means he loved them as long as they did what he wanted. Heaven help them if they didn't! What would have happened to you if I hadn't given in?'

'You really expect me to believe that he'd have had me locked up?'

'That was what Vanzani said.'

'Then why didn't Vanzani tell me that himself?'

'How can I know? Maybe he was too scared to tell you everything about Arturo's behaviour. He might have thought you wouldn't like it.'

Rico thought of his meeting with Vanzani in the early hours of that morning. The man had been shaking with nerves, had repeated himself, contradicted himself. He certainly hadn't been in a hurry to lay blame on Arturo Forza. Not to Arturo's grandson.

Certain vague memories of his childhood whispered past Rico: things half-seen, things fully seen but only half-understood, disjointed words that trailed into silence, glances quickly averted. Fear on people's faces. Fear in their voices. For a moment, the miasma of mistrust that had surrounded his grandfather seemed to choke him again.

'He said you would be locked up if I didn't cooperate,' Julie repeated. 'Maybe it was an idle threat. Should I have taken that chance with your safety?'

She saw the uncertainty in his face. He couldn't be quite sure. But that didn't mean he believed her.

'I know he was a hard man,' Rico said slowly.

'What did he say when you told him about us?'

'He was delighted. He said it was time I settled down and he looked forward to meeting you. He even asked me your favourite flowers so that he could fill the house to welcome you.'

'And you weren't suspicious?'

'I was surprised at his welcome. We'd parted on bad terms when I insisted on coming to England. But he greeted me with smiles...'

He stared at her.

'While he was smiling at you, he was sending Vanzani to bully me,' Julie told him. 'Vanzani walked in and took me by surprise. He made me write that letter, then he forced me to leave with him at once. He kept me in an hotel for a week, watching my every move in case I tried to contact you. He must have had someone watching our rooms to see when you returned.'

'I looked for you like a madman, but nobody knew where you'd gone,' Rico said sombrely. 'When I despaired of finding you, I came home to Italy. My grandfather was all sympathy—'

'Of course. He'd got what he wanted. Rico, didn't you know what he was like?'

'I knew he was ruthless, but this—my God! No, I don't believe it. This is a tale to justify yourself.'

'Vanzani snatched your locket from my neck. It left a mark that's still there. Look.'

She pulled aside the fawn silk of her shirt, revealing a faint line on the side of her neck where the chain had cut her. Frowning, Rico came close. He raised his hand and she felt the faint touch of one finger.

Light as it was, it caused a tremor deep within her. He was dreadfully near. For a moment, their faces almost touched. Then he drew back sharply.

'How do I know when that mark was made?' he demanded. 'You would say whatever suited you.'

'And of course you can't take my word for anything, can you?' she asked quietly.

'Do you expect me to?'

'Yes. At first you didn't believe your grandfather sent Vanzani to me, but now you know that's true.'

'He sent him to buy you off, that's all I know. You named a high price and took it. You gave my son to strangers and lived on blood money while you established your career.'

'No!'

'Don't lie to me. I know too much.'

'You know nothing,' she said desperately.

'Years ago, I set a team of inquiry agents onto the case. It took them time to track down Patsy Brown because the name was so common. Eventually they discovered that a Patsy Brown had given birth to a son at a hospital in a northern city, seven months after I last saw you. But then she vanished into thin air. Now I know it was because you'd changed your name.

'It took them years to pinpoint Julie Hallam as the same person. She lived in London, in Mayfair—the fashionable area, very expensive. And she lived alone. No sign of a child. But then she changed address and they lost her again. That was why I had to proceed through your agent.'

Julie turned away to hide her relief that Rico's spies hadn't been more efficient. She didn't live in Mayfair. Her home was Aunt Cassie's cottage in a modest London suburb. But she'd once stayed in Mayfair for two months, in a friend's borrowed flat, to be near a demanding engagement.

Aunt Cassie had taken Gary to visit friends in Scotland, too far for Julie to visit. If they'd watched her for those two months, they could easily have thought she was childless and lived alone.

Her press cuttings wouldn't have helped them, either. She'd refused several requests for interviews at home. Journalists were allowed to meet her at work or not at all, and she'd always kept Gary's existence a secret.

'I was determined to get you here and make you tell me what became of my son,' Rico continued. 'If you don't know his whereabouts, tell me the names of the authorities who acted in the matter. I'll contact them myself. He was adopted without my consent. I'll go to law—'

'Rico, it wasn't like that—'

'How old was he when you gave him away? Or didn't you give him? Did more money change hands?'

'How dare you!' she breathed.

'I dare say anything because I don't know you. You could be capable of any depravity.'

'Could be,' she echoed, facing him steadily. 'But do you really think I am?'

He looked at her desperately for a long moment. 'How do I know?' he asked hoarsely. 'Where is my son?'

'Leave him, Rico. There'll be other sons for you.'

'Are you mad? He's my first-born. Can't you understand what that means?'

'He was my first-born, too, and I want what's best for him. I want him to be happy. Could he be happy here, growing up to be another Forza, thinking of nothing but power and money? I want better for him than that.'

Rico's eyes narrowed. 'You have great courage to defy me.'

'I learned courage at the hands of your family. There's only one way with bullies. Stand up to them.'

His face was very pale. 'Does that include me?'

'If necessary.'

'You talk of power, but you have no idea how truly powerful I am. I wonder how long you think you can hold out against me.'

'What will you do, Rico? Threaten to have me locked up? And when that fails—what then?'

'I don't fail,' he said, his eyes kindling. 'As you will discover.'

'I'm not afraid of you.'

'Then you are very foolish,' he said in a voice that was deadly quiet.

'I don't want a battle, but if you force me to fight, I will.'

'And how many weapons have you? Only one. Your stubbornness. And that can be overcome. I have more weapons than you can dream of. Come, it'll be better for you to simply do what I want. You won't regret it. I know how to be generous when I'm pleased.'

His voice had grown softer. His dark eyes were hypnotic, forcing her to look only at him and forget the world. Now she knew how he ruled, by silently taking control of an opponent. He wanted her to think that she had no will but his, and she could almost believe it.

'Patsy...' he murmured.

'Don't call me Patsy,' she said unsteadily. 'I'm not Patsy any more.'

'Are you so sure of that? I'm not. I, too, thought Patsy was dead until I held you in my arms yesterday.'

'That—that shouldn't have happened,' she whispered.

'It was always meant to happen. From the moment you vanished from my life, it was inevitable that we would find each other again. You know that's true.'

'I—'

'Did you think you would go through the world and never meet me again, never kiss me again, never feel me kiss you? Some things are meant to be.'

As soon as he said it, she knew he was right. Some things were meant to be, and it was as inevitable as the moon and stars that one day she would be in his arms again.

She didn't know when he moved or when his hands first touched her shoulders, drawing her to him. It wasn't wise to melt against him as though the years had never been, but nothing could have stopped her.

She'd armoured her heart against her memories, but no armour could protect her from the real man, so close, so warm.

Yesterday he'd kissed her as a cruel assertion of power, but today he was as uncertain as herself. Patsy or Julie? He wasn't sure which woman he held in his arms. Or both?

She moved her lips against his, softly. She knew what happened next. His arms would go right around her in a gesture that enfolded and protected her. He would hold her against his heart, telling her that there, and there only, she belonged.

But not now. He kept his hands on her shoulders from where he could either draw her close or fend her off. He, too, had crafted armour to protect his heart. He was afraid. She sensed it. Afraid because his life was built around control, and it was slipping away.

But she, too, was afraid. An uprush of caution made her tense against him, pulling back to study his face. A stranger looked back at her; he had Rico's face and Rico's passion, but he was a stranger.

'No,' she protested, pulling away. 'Rico, stop this, please. We can't be at daggers drawn one minute and in each other's arms the next.'

'It seems that we can. But you're right. It shouldn't happen. We must...' He stepped back sharply and ran a hand distractedly through his hair. 'Many times, I imagined what it would be like meeting you again,' he said at last. 'But things don't always work out the way you plan.'

'I dreamed of our meeting, too,' she confessed. 'But I never thought of this. You've lived in my mind as you were then. I forgot that people move on.'

'And you've lived in my mind as a cruel betrayer. Now I find that partly untrue. But only partly...'

Suddenly Julie couldn't face talking any more. Since she arrived, she'd been in a state of continuous strain, and it was catching up with her now.

'I'm tired,' she said. 'I need to rest before this afternoon. I'd like to go to my dressing-room.'

'It isn't quite ready. You can rest here.' Rico indicated a leather couch.

He began to go round the huge windows, closing the shutters one by one, until the room was sunk in a soft, shadowy light. Outside, the fierce heat of Rome was at its height, but inside, all was peace and quiet.

'You won't be disturbed,' he said, then walked out before she could say anything.

Julie felt totally drained. All she wanted to do was lie down and let the tensions fall away. The leather couch was surprisingly comfortable and she stretched out on it, her hand over her eyes. In a few moments, she was dozing.

Her dreams were confused. Again she was in the plane that had brought her here, but the plane was attached to a thread. And on the other end was Rico, drawing her in, the catch he'd planned and schemed for.

His lips were on hers, kissing her ruthlessly, but then the years fell away and he was a boy, kissing her with reverence, whispering, 'I am yours, always.' They couldn't be the same man, but they were.

Then the dream grew very strange, for she dreamed that she half opened her eyes and through her eyelashes thought she could see Rico sitting beside her, watching her closely. He looked vulnerable, baffled.

He leaned towards her. 'Julie,' he said softly. 'Julie.'

'I've missed you so much,' she whispered. 'So many long years without you. So many nights I cried, but you weren't there.'

'Hush.' He laid a finger over her lips as though what she was saying hurt him too much to bear. 'The nights were long for me, too.'

She thought his lips brushed lightly against hers, but then the dream faded into darkness.

CHAPTER FIVE

WHEN she awoke, she lay for a while, thinking, wondering what was true and what fantasy. She could almost feel Rico's lips brushing against hers, no stronger than a whisper. But that was the power of dreams. They could seem so real even when it was only your own lonely heart producing the illusion.

But when she saw him again, she would know.

She yawned and stretched, feeling better. A woman in her fifties, with a kind of austere beauty, looked in. 'I am Galena, Signor Forza's secretary,' she said. 'I have brought you some coffee.'

Her calm maturity made her seem strangely out of place in these glitzy surroundings, and Julie asked, 'Have you worked for Signor Forza very long?'

'Only two years. Before that, I worked for his grandfather.'

'You knew Arturo Forza?' Julie asked quickly.

'*Sì*. Many years,' Galena said fervently. 'He was a great man.'

Julie knew that some people were fascinated by authority, however cruel. Obviously Galena was one of them.

'Tell me about him,' she invited. She sensed that Arturo was one of the keys to understand Rico.

The secretary left the room and returned with a large book. 'This is mine,' she said. 'I collected every word ever written about him.'

It was a scrapbook full of press cuttings. Curiously

Julie leafed through it. Nothing she found changed her opinion of Arturo Forza as a man who was coldly ruthless, sly, scheming and brutal.

At the end, she found a magazine feature, written when he died. It described the passing of 'a man cast in the mould of the ancient Roman emperors: a man of stern will and all-embracing vision'.

He came from a people that once ruled the known world, and the pride of that conquest still lived in him. In its own way, his financial empire was as mighty as the land empire that the Romans won by force centuries ago. His power stretched into many countries and affected millions of lives.

The writer then turned to Rico, Arturo's only relative, calling him 'the rebel', heir to banking millions but with no interest in banking. He owned shares in a film company, and starlets flocked to be seen on his arm. Women came and went. None seemed able to hold his volatile interest. He travelled, investing in different enterprises, always making money, then shrugging and moving on.

There emerged a picture of a restless man, not at ease with the world or himself. An unhappy man, seeking something he couldn't find, mourning a loss for which there were no words.

It struck Julie that she was the only person who understood that loss. Rico had had no child to put baby arms about his neck and fall asleep sweetly against him. She'd known a joy to compensate for her own grief, but for him, nothing. Could she blame him for what he'd become?

Suddenly her fears seemed exaggerated. She would

tell Rico about Gary and get Cassie to bring the boy
out to Italy. As he got to know his son, his heart would
soften and perhaps…perhaps…

The past was over, but surely the future might yet
be sweet?

To her disappointment, there was no sign of Rico
at the afternoon rehearsal. But when she'd finished, a
messenger slipped a note into her hands. It said simply, 'Nine-thirty this evening. We're going out on the
town. Rico.'

By now she was used to his abrupt commands, but
this time she wasn't offended. The feel of his kiss had
lingered with her all afternoon. She longed to see him
again. And there was in this note some hint of the boy
he'd once been, who loved to tease her with surprises.

That evening, she took loving care over her appearance, choosing a dress of white silk chiffon that
swept her ankles, and dainty silver jewellery. She was
sufficiently dressed up to be elegant, but this wasn't
the full professional gloss that she would have applied
for a singing engagement. Tonight she would be only
a woman enjoying the company of a man who could
still touch her heart. It was absurd that her pulse still
raced at the thought of meeting him, but she couldn't
help herself.

He was waiting for her in the foyer, wearing a dinner jacket and bow-tie. He smiled and kissed her hand,
and she thought she saw something warm and ardent
in his eyes.

He led her out of the hotel, gesturing towards something that stood by the kerb. Julie gave a little cry of
delight at the sight of a *carrozza*, one of the horse-
drawn carriages that plied their trade on the streets
of Rome.

'Ours for the evening,' Rico said, smiling.

'Oh, it's just as you…' She bit back the rest of the words. In their blissful youth, he'd promised to take her around Rome in a *carrozza*. Perhaps it wasn't tactful to remind him of that now.

But his eyes said he remembered.

He handed her in and she settled back happily against the leather upholstery. It was a light vehicle, with two large wheels and one shaggy black horse between the shafts. When they were seated, the driver started up. In a few moments, they were heading down the Via Veneto, the horse trotting steadily, unfazed by the clamorous traffic.

'You thought I'd forgotten, didn't you?' Rico asked her. 'I promised you this long ago.'

'I thought you might have chosen not to remember,' Julie said, picking her words with care.

'Tonight we cease hostilities,' he said. 'We think only that we are friends who have met again after too long apart.'

'That would be nice,' she agreed.

But was it really possible to be friends with a man of such vibrant sexual magnetism when her heart and body had come totally alive to him again? She had never seen him look more handsome than he did sitting beside her now.

'One may choose not to remember,' he said, taking up her words, 'but it isn't always a matter of choice.'

'No,' she agreed, 'it isn't.'

Darkness had fallen, and the city was coming to life in a different way from daytime. Brilliant light streamed out from windows and doors while strings of coloured lamps illuminated pavement cafés, winking off crystal and silver. And every building of note was bathed in floodlight.

Now was her chance to see some of the great monuments of Rome. The Castel Sant' Angelo, the huge old fortress prison on the banks of the River Tiber, came looming up, sinister and beautiful in floodlight, as they crossed the river. And there was St. Peter's, magical down the long vista of the Via della Conciliazione. Julie watched it in breathless silence, feeling her heart begin to grow content again in the warm night air.

Enraptured though she was, she never stopped being conscious of Rico or the fact that he was watching her intently.

Then they were moving out of the centre of the city and rising gradually until they reached a small inn, with tables set out under the stars. The landlord was expecting them and ushered them to a table by a wooden railing, with a view over the whole of the city.

The table was laid for two, with wine already uncorked. Rico had gone to a great deal of trouble, Julie realized.

'I promised you this, too,' he said, holding out her chair.

'"We will sup nectar and dine with the gods,"' she quoted wistfully. '"And Rome will be ours."'

'I was thinking of this very spot when I said that,' he said, seating himself opposite her. 'When I was a boy, I used to run away up here. I would look at the view and feel like an emperor. What is it?' he added, frowning for a shadow had crossed her face.

'Nothing,' Julie said quickly.

'Yes, tell me.'

'It's just that…it gives me a strange feeling when

you talk about your boyhood. It reminds me that everything you told me before was a—left a good deal out.'

'Was a lie.' He supplied the word she hadn't wanted to use.

'I didn't mean it like that,' she hastened to respond. 'But it was a shock to discover that what I believed about you simply wasn't true. It was like discovering that you'd been nothing but a ghost all the time.'

'I was so immature then,' he said thoughtfully. 'It never occurred to me that my harmless pretence—as I thought of it—was a kind of dishonesty.'

'What made you come to England and live as you did?'

Rico gave a wry grin, whose mockery was directed at himself. 'I'd been raised in luxury, so naturally I rebelled against it. I thought I was a big, independent man, rejecting the comfort I'd always known and living by my own efforts. I believed there was something noble in working for a pittance. Of course, I was only playing. If I hadn't been so young, I'd have seen that.

'But I was defying the powerful Arturo Forza and I was very proud of that. He was so angry that he even cut me off without a penny, which I thought was very adventurous.'

'So you knew what he was like?'

'I suppose I did,' he answered thoughtfully. 'Talking to you has brought back so many things I'd forgotten. He could smile and seem all benevolence, but behind the scenes he was always pulling strings. He used to tell me, "Once Romans ruled the world by military might. Now there are other ways to rule."

'If I wanted affection, I sought it from our cook. I

told you about her. I called her Nonna—Grandmother—because I loved her. I used to pretend that
she was my real nonna.'

'So all that was true?'

'About her teaching me to cook? Yes, that was true.
I was never so happy as when I was in the kitchen,
telling her all my childish troubles. To this day, there
are certain kitchen smells—garlic, paprika—that make
me feel good.'

His eyes were glowing with reminiscence. For the
first time, she saw him relaxed and at ease, as he had
once been all the time.

'Of course,' he added drily, 'Grandfather disap-
proved of my spending so much time with a "ser-
vant". I wanted to get away from his kind of thinking.
Now I remember. That was Nonna's idea. "Go some-
place where the air is cleaner", she told me. So I came
to London, took any unskilled job I could find and felt
free and happy for the first time in my life. And
then—'

'Stop,' Julie said suddenly. 'Don't say any more.'

Looking into her face, he understood. Any mention
of their happiness led remorselessly to their grief, and
she didn't want to remember that now. Neither did he.
He wanted to enjoy the flickering candlelight on her
face.

When he first saw her the other night, he'd thought
how changed she was. But now, in the soft lighting,
watching the pleading look she'd turned on him as she
begged him not to tread on dangerous ground, he
thought her miraculously unaltered. How young and
vulnerable she looked—as she had always looked.

The landlord appeared and served them with *strac-
ciatella*, a soup made with chicken, eggs, Parmesan

cheese and a little magic. Julie tasted it and gasped.
'But this—'

'Is the first thing I ever cooked for you,' he said
with a grin. 'You said you'd died and gone to heaven.
Wait till you see the next course.'

'Don't tell me,' she said eagerly. 'Let me guess.
That thing you made after our first quarrel—'

'We never quarrelled,' he said at once. 'We had
small unimportant tiffs, which were all my fault. But
after the first one, I made something special to show
you how sorry I was.'

'Macaroni with ham and eggs.'

'That's right.'

'But, Rico, you haven't—'

'I ordered a special menu tonight, hoping it would
please you.'

She was awed by the trouble he'd taken, and the
delicious food cast the spell that he'd obviously in-
tended. She was whisked back to their attic as though
on a magic carpet. But this time there was no sadness
in the memories. Macaroni to make up their tiff, followed by Roman beef stew, 'because I love you more
than my life, *carissima*.'

He'd made love to her with his hands and his loins,
but he'd also seduced her with his cooking. It all came
back now in a blaze of delight.

'You eat ice cream like a little girl,' he said when
she was on the sweet course. 'As though it was a big
treat and you were afraid someone was coming to
snatch it away.'

'Someone always did when I was a child. My
brother grabbed everything he wanted. Being able to
eat ice cream without looking over my shoulder was
really a treat.'

There in her mind was the ice-cream parlour, just around the corner from their little home, where he'd taken her one evening. She'd been dazed at the variety of flavours on offer, but Rico had been loftily dismissive.

'One day I'll take you to Italy, where we really know how to make ice cream,' he'd boasted. 'This is nothing. But it will do for now.'

How tenderly he'd laughed as she tried to decide between the merits of pineapple and pistachio, mint and chocolate, strawberry, banana—the list went on for ever. His wallet had been full of a hard-earned bonus.

'*Rico, that's all the money from your overtime.*'

'*How better could I spend it than on you, piccina?*'

Now she looked up and saw the same memory in his eye. Neither of them spoke. They didn't have to.

'My plate's empty,' she said with meaning.

'Let's see what else they've got.' He looked around for a waiter, but there were none in sight. 'I'll find someone.'

While she waited, Julie glanced over to a nearby patch of grass, where the *carrozza* stood. The horse had his nose in a water trough, and the elderly driver was leaning back, looking up at the stars. Impulsively Julie took a clean glass, filled it with wine and went over to them.

'*Grazie,*' the old man said, accepting the glass. He held it up.

'*Salute!*'

'*Salute!*' She raised her own glass to meet his.

The horse finished drinking and snorted noisily.

'He looks quite old,' she said. 'What's his name?'

'Miko,' the driver said. 'He's nearly twenty. He's

earned a rest but...' He shrugged, and Julie guessed
he couldn't afford to retire the old horse. She stroked
its long nose.

'I usually only work him during the day,' the driver
went on. 'My cousin was supposed to do this job, but
his horse went lame. It's good money. We can't afford
to lose it.'

'You mean Miko has already done a day's work?'
Julie asked in dismay. He nodded. 'Poor old thing,'
she murmured. 'I thought he was making heavy
weather of that hill.'

She saw Rico searching for her, holding a plate
piled high with ice cream. Smiling, she joined him.

'You were right,' she said when she'd scraped the
plate. 'Italy does make the best ice cream in the
world.'

'If you've finished, we can go now. I have still
much to show you.'

Miko stood patiently as they climbed into the *carrozza*, but Julie was glad for his sake that this time the
way was downhill. Soon they found themselves trotting through narrow backstreets, where yellow lamps
glowed on the cobblestones.

'Where are we going now?' she asked.

'To the Trevi Fountain. That's another place I promised to show you.'

But it seemed that Miko had other ideas. Without
warning, he tried to swerve left, and it took all the
driver's efforts to keep him going straight.

'*Scusi*,' he apologized when they had come to a
halt. 'That's the way home.'

Julie jumped down, ran to Miko's head and patted
his nose soothingly. The old horse stood docilely,
watching her out of beautiful brown eyes. 'You poor

old thing,' she said. 'You've had such a long day.'
She spoke to Rico, who'd followed her. 'We don't
need them any more, do we?'

'I'm being paid for the whole evening, *signorina*,'
the driver said nervously. 'There are another two
hours—'

'Rico, can't we take a taxi and let them go home?'

'Of course,' Rico said at once. He handed some
money to the driver. 'Thank you. You can go now.'

The old man's eyes widened as he saw the amount.
He peeled off some notes and tried to return them to
Rico, who waved them away.

'It was the agreed fee,' he said. '*Buona notte*.'

'*Grazie, signorina*,' the driver said fervently to
Julie. 'Eh, Miko! Home to bed.' He slapped the reins,
and they were gone.

'Why are you looking at me like that?' Julie asked,
for Rico was regarding her with a tender half smile.

'The landlord of The Crown had a dog that liked to
drink beer,' he said. 'The regulars thought it was a
great joke to get the poor creature drunk, until you hit
the roof. You called them a bunch of no-good louts,
and you told the landlord that he should be ashamed
of himself.

'I thought he was going to fire you on the spot, but
you didn't care. You just waded in, and nobody ever
saw that dog in the bar again.'

'What's that got to do with tonight?'

'Everything,' he said, slipping an arm about her
shoulder and beginning to walk. 'Everything.'

They were closer to the centre of Rome than she'd
realized, and after they'd strolled through a few streets,
she heard the sound of cascading water. The next mo-

ment, they turned a corner and the glory of the Trevi Fountain burst upon her.

It was huge. At its apex towered the god of the ocean, his chariot borne by marine horses, plunging and swooping in and out of the water. At every point, water gushed out into the great basin, its droplets shining, the noise so loud that Rico had to raise his voice to talk.

'Here.' he gave her a coin and turned her so that her back was to the fountain. 'You must toss it over your shoulder and make a wish to return to Rome.'

But how could she make such a wish? She'd sworn that when she left here, she would never come back, never risk seeing Rico Forza again. How could she return, unless…?

Taking a deep breath, she closed her eyes, tossed the coin over her shoulder and wished.

'Did you make the wish?' he asked.

'Maybe.'

'Did you wish anything else? Most people do.'

'That would be telling,' she teased.

She felt light-headed with happiness. The journey from sadness to joy had been so swift that it left her giddy. It seemed too good to be true that Rico's heart should have melted towards her so suddenly.

Too good to be true.

She pushed the uneasy thought aside, telling herself not to be suspicious.

From somewhere nearby, Julie could hear the sound of an accordion. They followed the music and found a little café in a cul-de-sac. Couples were dancing in the street, and Rico took her into his arms.

'Do you remember that tune?' he asked as they moved dreamily in time to the music. 'It was an Italian

song, and I taught it to you. At least, I tried. You were
very uncomplimentary about my voice.'

She laughed. 'I said you sounded like a corncrake.'

'And you wrote your own words to the song and
sang it in the pub that night.'

'So I did.' It was coming back to her. The tune was
fragile, almost nothing, the kind of thing that belonged
in a music box, with a little revolving figure. She'd
picked up that echo at once and built a pretty fantasy
around it.

She began to sing in a soft, murmuring voice.

'The world is turning again and again,
Everything comes around.
Sleeping or waking, loving or sighing,
Never ending, never beginning,
Round and round it goes.
Still I keep turning again and again,
Never know when to stop.
Loving you, missing you, hoping and hurting,
Never remembering, never forgetting,
Round and round I go.
My heart is turning again and again,
You never let it go.
Holding me, leaving me, calling me, grieving me,
Never beginning, never ending,
Round and round we go,'

'Fancy you remembering the words after all this
time,' he said.

'I remember everything. I've tried not to, but—
you're right. It isn't a matter of choice.'

Suddenly she was crying. She didn't know where
the tears had come from, but they were pouring down

her cheeks as though the grief of years had distilled into this one moment.

'Julie!' he said, horrified.

'We were children,' she wept. 'We thought because we were in love the world had to be ours.'

'We made our own world,' he whispered against her hair.

'Yes, and we fooled ourselves that it was the real world. But it wasn't like that. It couldn't be.'

'Don't cry,' he pleaded. 'Look up at me.'

She did, and found his lips caressing hers tenderly. His hand was gentle beneath her head. She felt herself melting. All her hard-won caution couldn't win out against the emotions that lived in her, only for him.

His mouth was as she remembered—full, sensuous, ardent. But above all, hers. The first night he'd kissed her cruelly, coldly, asserting possession and authority. But now, miraculously, after all that had passed, he kissed like a boy, breathless with first love. She gave him a heartfelt answer and felt his response in the tightening of his arms, the increasing intensity of his breathing.

'Mia piccina,' he murmured. 'Do you remember when I used to call you that?'

'I remember everything,' she said fervently.

'And so do I. I've tried to forget, but you were always there. There was always this.'

On the last word, he smothered her mouth again. Now all uncertainty was gone and he was the passionately possessive lover, reclaiming what he had never truly relinquished.

Here in the public street, they could kiss without fear of being noticed because many other couples were doing the same. It was a place for lovers and a night for lovers. And they were lovers again, as they had always been.

'Let me come back with you,' he whispered. 'I want to stay with you tonight. Please.'

'Rico…' She looked at him in wonder.

'We've been apart too long, *mio amore*. Don't you feel that, too?'

'I've never wanted to be apart from you and I've thought about you every moment of the past eight years.'

He took her hand. 'Come with me. Now the parting is over and the love can begin again.'

CHAPTER SIX

Rico led her out of the side-street and close to the Trevi Fountain.

'There's a *carrozza* rank just around the corner,' he said. 'We can take one back to the hotel. What is it?' For Julie had freed her hand.

'You go on and get the *carrozza*,' she said. 'There's something I want to do first.'

She watched him go, feeling as though she might burst with happiness. What she'd longed for had happened. Rico's heart was open to her again in trust. She could tell him everything about their son, bring the boy out to meet him. She drew in her breath at the thought of that meeting and what might result from it.

It was still a risk. He might be angry at the way she'd kept Gary hidden. But the prize was a happy future for the three of them together, and it dazzled her. And she would protect herself against the risk by a tiny superstition.

She turned back to the Trevi Fountain. Rico had said that most people uttered a second wish, and this would be hers: that Rico would receive her revelations in the right way.

She took out a coin, kissed it, closed her eyes and tossed it over her shoulder, wishing with all her heart.

And then something very strange happened. Opening her eyes again, she found herself looking straight at a man whose face was familiar. He turned away so quickly that she was puzzled. It was almost as if he'd been watching her but didn't want to be noticed himself.

She looked around, and there was another familiar face on one side and yet a third on the other. They, too, stepped back into the shadows to avoid her glance.

Oh, no! she thought. I'm imagining things. He wouldn't do that. But a prickle went up her spine as she recognized the dreadful truth. She'd seen these men at La Dolce Notte. They all worked for Rico.

Suddenly the monstrous situation was clear to her. While her heart had been melting to him, he'd had her watched by his hired heavies. Spied on like an enemy because, to him, that's what she was.

Nothing about tonight was real. The whole evening, so beautiful until this moment, had been a set-up. Rico had sweet-talked her, making love with his eyes, his choice of food and a certain note in his voice, recalling the past in order to seduce her into a compliant mood.

He'd succeeded frighteningly well. And now the stage was set for the last act of the comedy. Then, lying in bed in his arms, overwhelmed by passion, she would tell him what he wanted to know. That was how he'd planned it.

Too good to be true! Some corner of her mind where reason still lived had called out the warning that her heart had refused to heed. Believing him because she longed to do so, she'd come within a hair's breadth of falling for his cruel scheme.

She'd thought she knew bitterness before, but now she realized she'd barely tasted it. The sense of betrayal made her giddy.

Rico was approaching, the *carrozza* just behind

him. He held out his hands to her, smiling. 'Let's go now,' he said. 'This is a wonderful night.'

'Yes, it is,' she said steadily. 'And I'll tell you what's wonderful about it. This is the night when my eyes were finally opened.'

'What do you mean by that?' he asked.

'I fooled myself that part of you was still the man I loved. But that man would never have hired guards to keep me in view while he was acting as though...' She was unable to go on. She couldn't put into words what the evening had meant to her.

Rico's face darkened, and he swore under his breath. 'Please, this wasn't meant to happen—'

'No, I wasn't supposed to notice them, was I?'

'I meant—I was going to call them off.'

'Am I watched everywhere I go?'

'Before this—yes. But if you'd only—'

'I wonder what exactly their job is, Rico? Make sure I don't escape or just report if I make any phone calls? After all, whoever runs the hotel switchboard must have told you by now that I never use the phone in my room.'

He stood silent under her accusations. He had no answer for them.

'How could you do it?' she breathed. 'No, don't try to tell me. I don't want to know.'

'Julie, please, I'm sorry you found out this way—'

'Yes, it shuts off one of your options, doesn't it?' she demanded angrily. 'After this, I won't fall for the "You've always lived in my heart" line.'

Even in this poor light, she could see that he was as white as a sheet. Whatever he'd meant to happen, this was distressing him. She didn't care. She wanted to hurt him as dreadfully as he had hurt her.

'How far were they meant to follow us, Rico? Into my hotel suite? Perhaps they'd have hidden behind the sofa while we—'

'Stop it!' he said harshly. 'It wasn't what you—well, we'll talk about that later.'

'We'll never talk about it. After this, please stay out of my way. Good night.'

Before he knew what she meant to do, she turned and darted away down a side-street. In a moment, she was lost in the darkness.

The three men who'd been watching made a move to go after her but were halted by a look from Rico. He stood there scowling while the *carrozza* driver jumped down and came to the horse's head, looking questioningly at Rico.

'Take it away.'

'The *signorina*...?'

'I said take it away,' Rico snapped, tossing him some money.

The driver allowed himself a small grin. A man whose woman had walked out on him in public was an object of derision. Then he saw the dangerous little pulse that beat at the corner of Rico's mouth and his grin faded. He grabbed the money, jumped aboard and fled.

Rico knew what kind of a figure he cut. His own henchmen had witnessed his being made to look a fool, but they were too wise to get near him. They understood very well the cold menace in his eyes.

He dismissed them with a curt nod and returned to the hotel on foot. He needed the walk to calm his fury: fury at Julie for treating him with contempt, fury with himself for having handled matters badly.

The receptionist confirmed that she was upstairs. He

went up and rapped on her door. When there was no reply, he rapped again.

'Please go away,' came her voice. 'I've gone to bed.'

'Then you can get up again and talk to me,' he said grimly.

'I have no wish to talk to you, now or ever.'

'Open this door!'

'No.'

He controlled himself.

'What happened tonight was unfortunate—'

'Is that your word for it?'

'I'm sorry you found out this way, but I must find my son, and you're the only person who can give me a lead. You have to. I'm in deadly earnest.'

'And I'm in earnest when I say that a man who acts like this is no fit father for my son. I won't help you find him, and if I have my way, he'll never so much as know you exist.'

'I'll tell you one more time. Open this door!'

'And I'm telling you for the last time. No!'

Rico drew a sharp breath. Nobody had defied him for years.

Then he heard a terrible sound. The faint unmistakable sound of a smothered laugh.

He whirled and saw a waiter moving away down the corridor. The man had undoubtedly heard more than enough. And he'd laughed. That made twice in one night that Julie had exposed him to derision.

'Damn you!' he said under his breath. 'Damn you for making a fool of me!'

Julie waited until Rico's footsteps had faded before she allowed herself to relax. She'd been standing against the door, so tense that her body ached, but even though her tension now drained away, she found she was still aching all over.

But her muscles could never ache as painfully as her heart.

She'd lied when she told Rico that she'd gone to bed. When she reached her room, she'd been unable to do anything but sit on her bed, shivering. She was still sitting there when he knocked. She'd forced herself to rise, and it had been almost a surprise to find that she could still walk.

When Rico had gone, she stayed leaning against the door without the strength to move. It was safe to cry now. She'd suppressed tears as long as there was a chance he might hear, but at this moment she felt as though she would weep forever.

She stripped off the lovely dress that she had donned so happily such a short time before. Her emotions raw, she looked back at that earlier self and realized how much senseless hope had been in her heart. She got under the shower, letting the water lave her. Here she could weep unrestrainedly and the cascading water would hide the sound.

All the carefully constructed defences of the years had been destroyed in one evening by his cynical manipulation. She'd sworn not to love Rico Forza because, if she wanted to keep sane and functioning, she couldn't afford to. But with a few soft words and false kisses, he'd returned her to the past when she was a vulnerable girl, adoring him with all the passion of first love.

And the feelings, once reawakened, wouldn't die. She couldn't kill her love with the knowledge of his betrayal.

She'd heard that love and hate were two sides of the same coin. Now she knew it was true.

To her relief, there was no sign of Rico at rehearsal next morning. After her disillusionment of the night before, she never wanted to see him again.

Carlo was ready for her, and they plunged into a lively session in which everything seemed to go right. Julie felt a little comforted. There had always been music to turn to when her life went wrong.

'I can't wait for your opening night,' Carlo said after finishing on a triumphant chord. 'You're going to knock them dead.'

'Well, if I do, the credit's yours,' she insisted. 'You keep pushing me to take risks.'

'And you bring them all off.'

They smiled together like conspirators. Julie's spirits rose and she thought she could even cope with Rico.

Then she saw him.

He'd appeared at the back of the club, accompanied by a young and very attractive woman. She had a dainty, curvaceous figure and a generous bosom, as an extremely low-cut sweater revealed. Her hair was piled high and elaborately on her head, and her exotic looks were emphasized by flamboyant make-up.

A chill wind seemed to shiver through Julie as the words of the magazine feature came back to her. Seldom seen without a starlet on his arm...the most beautiful women, his for the taking...

His for the taking. When she arrived, Rico had made it clear he considered that Julie was his for the taking. But last night, she'd struck back, forcing him to see her as a woman to be reckoned with. This was his retaliation.

Rico escorted his beautiful companion down to the stage and brought her over to Julie.

'Mariella, *cara*,' he said, 'I want you to meet Julie Hallam, the new star that everyone is talking about.'

Mariella made a sound between a simper and a giggle, then enveloped Julie in a scented embrace.

'I've been so longing to meet you,' she said. 'Rico has talked about nothing but Julie Hallam ever since he booked you. It's been Julie Hallam this and Julie Hallam that until I've almost been jealous.' She performed the simpering giggle again. 'Not really jealous, of course.'

'I'm sure you have no need,' Julie said politely. Inside her, a storm of dismay had seized her without warning and was whirling her about. She forced herself to smile and look composed.

'Well, that's what my Rico says,' Mariella tittered. 'He says, "*Carissima*, how could there be anyone for me but you?" And then he gives me something beautiful to show how much he loves me.'

'I'm sure he's very generous,' Julie murmured, hardly knowing what she was saying.

'Oh, all the time. Look at my new present.' She stretched out her wrist to display a gleaming emerald bracelet. 'He called me up last night and told me to meet him at our favourite jewellers in the Via Condotti. The shop was closed, but for him they opened up. And then he just swept me inside and told them to bring out their very best.' Her voice dropped. 'Do you know Rome?'

'I—no.'

'Then you don't know the Via Condotti. It's the

most expensive street in the city. The most luxurious jewellers and dressmakers are there, and my darling Rico has accounts with all of them. I simply order what I want. But it's best when the man takes you himself, don't you think?'

By now, Julie had herself in hand and was able to smile and say, 'I'm sure it is.'

She hadn't missed the significance of 'last night'. It could only mean that Rico had gone straight from her to Mariella; from one woman who gave him an uncomfortable glimpse of himself to another who would soothe his pride with flattery that he'd paid for. And after they'd left the jeweller? What then?

'Have you asked her?' Rico asked, coming over from where he'd been talking to Carlo.

Mariella shrieked with affected laughter. 'We've been so busy talking that I forgot. Julie, Rico and I are having a house-warming party the day after tomorrow. Simply everybody will be there. And to make it perfect, you must come and sing for us.'

Rico and I. A house-warming party. They lived together.

'You're very kind,' she said, 'but I'm saving my voice for the opening night. I'm sure you understand.'

Mariella's pout showed that she didn't understand anyone who said no. 'But you must,' she insisted. 'You must.'

'It's kind of you to ask me, but I'm afraid it's impossible,' Julie said firmly.

A faint noise came from the back. Somebody had arrived and attracted Mariella's butterfly attention. She gave a shriek and launched herself toward the newcomer in a cloud of frothy endearments.

'It's impossible,' Julie repeated.

'Surely not,' Rico said. 'I'm looking forward to hearing you sing in my house. I'm sure you won't disappoint me.'

'As I did last night, you mean?'

'The less said about last night the better. You chose to think the worst of me—'

'It wasn't very hard.'

'Now you can think whatever you like. Just do as I say.'

'Arturo Forza has spoken,' she flung at him.

'Do you think you insult me by likening me to him? You're mistaken. It makes me proud.'

'At one time, you'd have known it was an insult. You were a better man then, Rico.'

He took a step closer and spoke in an undertone. 'You dare say that? Who knows more than you what made me the man I am?'

'A man who'd lie to a woman who used to love him and thanks heaven that she doesn't any more. A man who'd use every trick and laugh up his sleeve while he fooled her.'

'I didn't—'

'Arturo would have been proud of you last night. What a pity it didn't work.'

'Yes, I was clumsy, wasn't I?' he said harshly.

'Don't worry. It didn't make any real difference. I wasn't going to give in even before I spotted your hired heavies. I've changed, too, you see. I've learned caution and suspicion. It would take a lot more than an evening's glib talk and a few false kisses to win me over.'

Pride and desperation drove her to utter what she said. 'Don't fool yourself that you were the only one playing games. I was very curious to know how far you'd go.'

A withered look crossed his face. 'You're lying.'

'Am I? Of course, you'd know about lying, wouldn't you.'

'What does that mean?'

'There are lies of omission. You never mentioned that you were living with Mariella.'

'Mariella has nothing to do with you and me.'

'There is no "you and me".'

He drew a sharp breath. 'It is pointless to discuss this. I wish you to sing at my house the day after tomorrow.'

She looked at him angrily. This was another demonstration of power, and it was cruel, vengeful.

'Rico, what are you playing at?' she said tightly.

'I don't play games. I'm giving an important function. People who matter to me commercially will be there, and I want the best. You will please attend to my wishes.'

'This wasn't in my contract. I sing at the club. I'm not yours to move around like a pawn.'

'I thought we'd already settled that you were. You owe me, Julie. Never forget that you owe me a huge debt. Let's just say that I'm claiming payment in my own way.'

'I don't want to do this,' she said desperately.

His smile was like ice. 'I'm sure you don't. But you'll do it.' He called to Mariella. 'It's all right, *carissima*. Julie has agreed to grace our party.'

'My God, I hate you,' she whispered.

'Then we're agreed about something. I've already given Carlo a list of what you will sing.'

He turned away, calling to Mariella. She came tittuping towards him, embraced him in a theatrical gesture, and they went out together.

On the day of the party, Carlo drove Julie to Rico's house on the Appian Way. They went in the early afternoon to allow time for a brief rehearsal and sound check, and Julie had leisure to observe the old tree-lined avenue.

'What are those buildings every few yards?' she asked Carlo. 'They're too small to be houses.'

'They're mausoleums,' Carlo replied. 'This road is over two thousand years old. The old aristocratic families built their tombs along here. And farther along are the catacombs where the early Christians used to hide.'

'Two thousand years,' Julie mused.

'Rome isn't called the Eternal City for nothing. The past is still here. When I get depressed, I think of all the people who have come and gone. In another thousand years, that's what we'll be—people who came and went.'

After a moment, Julie said, 'Do you mean anything special by that?'

'Rico's been on hot coals since he knew you were coming. Normally he's very cool about women. He can have all he wants, and none of them matter. But you've got him strung out.'

'What about Mariella?'

Carlo gave a snort. 'Mariella, Ginetta, Santuzza—they're all the same.'

'But isn't he living with her?'

'She'd like to think so. But she has her own apartment in the city. She goes to Rico's house when he snaps his fingers, then leaves when he tells her to.'

'Everybody does everything when he tells them to,' Julie said with a faint touch of bitterness. 'Arturo Forza's grandson.'

'Did you know the old man?' Carlo asked in surprise.

'No, but I—I've heard of him.'

'He was a real—' Carlo used a very expressive word. 'Rico is frighteningly like him. There was a time when I thought he might break out of Arturo's shadow, live his own life with human values, not commercial ones. But—I don't know—perhaps he still can.'

He waited to see if she would answer this. When she didn't, he began telling her who lived in the luxurious houses they were passing, and in this way they completed the journey.

Rico lived in a palatial villa set in extensive grounds. The building was three storeys high with a row of stone columns at the front. It was less a home than a palace for a prince, and Carlo confirmed that it had once belonged to an old aristocratic family.

'Arturo set his heart on it and got the family in a financial stranglehold. Then he tightened it until they sold at his price.'

'I can believe it,' Julie said.

At every turn, the evil old man had left his mark. He might be dead, but he was still a malign presence in her life.

'Why did Mariella call this a house-warming party if Rico inherited it from his grandfather?' she asked.

'He's renovated the picture gallery. There are some valuable paintings in the collection, and its reopening is an occasion.'

They climbed the broad stone steps to the entrance.

As soon as they were inside, Julie saw Rico and Mariella.

Although it was afternoon, the starlet was dressed to kill in a tight, low-cut dress and adorned with a mass of jewellery that would have been more suitable for evening. She was giving directions to servants in a sharp voice that contrasted dramatically with her usual breathless tones. One by one they scurried nervously away.

Mariella turned and spotted them, then immediately switched on her smile and flowed across the mosaic floor, hands outstretched in a parody of welcome.

'I'm so glad you managed to get here,' she cooed. 'We're all looking forward to your performance. Of course, you should really have used the rear door, but never mind.'

'Sorry,' Julie said, understanding this perfectly. 'Nobody told us where the tradesmen's entrance was.'

Mariella's smile wavered a fraction.

'Why should they?' Rico said, coming up behind her. 'You're not tradesmen.'

'We're the hired performers,' Julie reminded him. She could see that he was discomfited by Mariella's rudeness.

'You are my honoured guests,' he said firmly. 'Mariella, which room have you allocated to Julie?'

'Room? But why—'

'She will need somewhere to prepare for her performance.'

'But of course. She can use my room. I'll take her myself.'

As they went through the house, Mariella showed off its glories with a proprietary air. Her own bedroom was a lavish show-place, furnished in palatial style. It was dominated by a huge four-poster bed, which Mariella assured her was 'the most comfortable in the world'.

'The old mattress was rather lumpy,' she confided, 'and I told my Rico that I simply must have a new one. He said I should order anything I liked, so I called the store and told them I wanted "a bed for lovers". I think everything should be perfect for love. Don't you?'

Julie looked her in the eye. 'I think it takes a great deal more than a mattress to make love perfect. Thank you for your hospitality.'

Mariella flounced out without another word. Julie watched her go with a wry smile, but the smile faded when she was alone. It was easy to be amused by the starlet's stupidity and greed, but it didn't change the fact that she was here with Rico, flaunting her position as mistress of his house.

And it hurt, she realized. After all her brave thoughts about being finished with him, it still hurt to see him with another woman, hearing Mariella talk about 'My Rico' and boast about a lovers' bed.

Julie could have told her that if you were in the arms of the man you loved, it didn't matter if you were in an old iron bedstead with a mattress that was too narrow and full of lumps. She put a hand over her eyes, and for a moment her lips trembled.

After a while, she went down to find the picture gallery, her footsteps echoing on the mosaic floors. She felt dwarfed by the high ceilings and huge rooms with their lush frescoes, and suddenly she desperately needed some fresh air.

When she arrived on the ground floor, a faint breeze reached her, and she saw that a door to the garden stood open. She hurried through it with relief, then stopped, feeling as though she'd stepped back in time.

It was impossible but true.

She'd been here before.

CHAPTER SEVEN

SHE looked around wildly, trying to understand the shattering thing that had happened. How did she recognize the curve of that path? How could she know the shape of the fountain even before she saw it?

And then she caught her breath as the truth dawned.

Long ago, a man with the power of a Roman emperor had been photographed here with his grandson, a boy he was rearing to be like himself. And those pictures had been used to break the heart of the boy and the girl who loved him.

Everything that Vanzani had shown her lived in Julie's mind, engraved there by grief. Now she saw place after place that she remembered from the pictures, and a kind of horror rose in her.

She pulled herself together, refusing to give in to the feeling. She hadn't yet called Gary, and the privacy of this garden was her chance. Her mobile was in her bag, and after a quick look round to make sure she was alone, she dialled. In a few moments, she was talking to her son.

Thrilled to hear from her, he chatted eagerly about a boat trip he'd taken, the sights he'd seen and the present he'd bought her. Julie listened, a happy smile spreading over her face as tension was replaced by delight.

'Gary, listen,' she laughed, trying to break into his babbling talk. 'Gary—' When she could get a word in edgeways, she whispered the endearments that she knew he loved.

'I love you, Mommy,' he said.

'I...' She was about to say she loved him when an awareness of danger made her look up and stiffen.

Rico was standing nearby, watching her.

'Me, too,' she said quickly. 'I must go now. Bye.' She hung up.

'I hope you didn't shorten your conversation because of me,' he said. 'I'm sure "Gary" was desolate.'

'I said all that was necessary,' she replied stiffly.

'Of course, if he's madly in love with you, the cleverest thing you could do is hang up,' Rico observed ironically. 'Keep him wondering.'

'I should go inside. They'll be waiting for me.'

'Don't rush. I've looked forward to showing you my home.'

'Your lady friend has shown it to me, and I congratulate you on its magnificence,' Julie said, trying to leave.

He detained her with a hand. 'You don't sound very enthusiastic.'

'Maybe I just don't care for magnificence. It's a show-place, not a home.'

'Have you thought that it might have been yours?'

'Never,' she said at once. 'This place is poisoned. I couldn't have lived in it.'

'It was the home of my childhood.'

'And it poisoned you, too. How much, I wonder? How badly harmed had you been already when you came to live in London?'

Then he said something unexpected. 'Badly, perhaps. But you could have made me better. Happiness brings out the best in a man, and misery the worst.

Now we'll never know what might have happened.' He turned accusing eyes on her. 'Don't ask me such questions. Do you want me to hate you more?'

'Could you hate me more?'

'I thought I couldn't. I've thought that many times, but I always found new depths. Hatred is unending and bottomless. You taught me that lesson, not my grandfather, whom you try to blame for so much.'

She had nothing to say to that.

'Shall I show you the garden?' he asked politely.

'No need. I already know it very well. That fountain used to have two winged horses. One of them has been removed in the past few years. And you had a piebald pony that would put his front hoofs on the fountain edge. You loved that little horse. You used to put your arms right round him and press your face against his neck.'

'How the devil did you know that?' he asked, going pale.

'It was in the photographs Vanzani showed me. He'd brought them to demonstrate how far above me you were. So coming here now is like meeting ghosts. Maybe I'll meet your ghost round the next corner.'

'But I'm not dead.'

'Mariella keeps calling you "my Rico". She's welcome to you. My Rico died a long time ago.'

'Yes,' he said quietly. 'A long time ago. On the same day as Patsy Brown.'

'Rico, *caro*.'

Like people waking up from a dream, they turned to see Mariella waving and hurrying along the path towards them, her face hard with suspicion.

'Why do you waste your time with women like that?' Julie demanded in disgust.

'They make the best companions,' Rico said wryly. 'You always know where you are with them.'

He walked away to meet Mariella. Julie waited till they were gone before she returned to the house and found the picture gallery, which, luckily, was on a more human scale than the rest of the house. She and Carlo ran through a couple of songs, and Julie found the acoustics excellent.

'You'll meet Beppe in a minute,' Carlo told her. 'He's going to be second on the bill at La Dolce Notte, and he'll also be doing a song tonight.'

'I think I've heard of him.'

'He used to be a big star in Italy, but the fashion has rather passed him by. You'll like him.'

Julie did like him. Beppe was a roly-poly charmer. He had neither looks nor youth, but he did have a roguish twinkle in his eye that instantly captivated her. He greeted her with a wildly dramatic flourish, kissing her hand and presenting her with a red rose. She couldn't help laughing, which seemed to please him.

Carlo took Beppe through his song, but then the elderly singer had a surprise.

'Listen,' he said sitting at the piano. He sang 'Whatever Happened to My Heart?' His eyes invited her and she joined in. They sounded well together. 'We sing it tonight?' he asked.

'Why not?'

They tried it again, this time with Carlo at the piano. Beppe stood next to her, looking tenderly up into her eyes, for she was three inches taller. If he'd been a younger man, she couldn't have sung this song with him, but he was funny and irresistible.

When they finished, he embraced her, and Julie

hugged him back, laughing. But then she looked up and her laughter died.

Rico was standing there, his face as pale as death. For a moment, she thought he would speak to her, but instead he walked away.

Soon the important guests began to arrive for a banquet, followed by the entertainment. Julie declined to join the party. She didn't want to see him and Mariella together. Not that she cared what they did. She just didn't want to see it.

She showered in Mariella's ornate bathroom, then put on a towelling robe and prepared to take forty winks, as she usually did before a performance. Nothing would have persuaded her to lie down on the bed, but luckily there was a couch, long enough to stretch out on. She took a spare blanket from the closet, set her small travelling alarm to wake her in an hour and lay back, taking deep breaths.

But she couldn't sleep. She was haunted by Rico's voice saying, 'You could have made me better.'

She'd been little more than a child, struggling against monstrous forces that were too strong for her. She'd paid the price and lived with it. But the price that Rico had paid almost made her believe that she'd given in too easily. And betrayed him.

She covered her face with her hands, refusing to think such thoughts in case she went mad.

There was a sharp rap on her door. Rubbing her eyes, she went to open it. Rico stood outside, handsome and severe in a dinner jacket.

'I shan't keep you long,' he said, walking in and turning to confront her. His face was austere. 'I told you the other day what you were to sing. Beppe also has his instructions. I wish you to keep to that programme with no alterations. None at all.'

'Whatever…?' she began to say.

Then she remembered Rico watching her with Beppe. And listening to the song they'd sung together.

'On my first day, you virtually ordered me to sing that song,' she objected.

'Alone,' he said in an iron voice. 'I do not consider it suitable for a duet.'

Except when sung by a boy and girl, brilliant with the joy of youthful passion, her caressing tones struggling with his tuneless grating so that they both laughed. And laughter melted into love.

'You're right,' she said after a moment. 'It never was suitable for a duet. I'll tell Carlo and Beppe.'

'I've already done so.'

He inclined his head curtly and was about to leave when his gaze fell on the couch with its rumpled blanket.

'I'm sure Mariella wouldn't have minded your using her bed,' he observed.

She didn't answer except with her eyes. He understood. After a moment, he left the room.

That night, she sang with a hundred priceless paintings looking down on her from the walls, and her performance was a tremendous success. She had a perfect view of Rico and Mariella sitting together in the front row, but after the first glance she didn't look at them again. The members of the audience were well fed, content with their money and status, and ready to enjoy themselves. The room resounded with their cheers.

Afterwards she refused Rico's invitation to remain and join the party, although Carlo and Beppe accepted. 'I'd rather have an early night,' she said.

'In that case, my chauffeur will take you home.'

She collected her things, and by the time she was downstairs, the car was waiting. Rico handed her in, thanked her again and said good-night. His manner was cool. They might have been no more than distant acquaintances. But he stood on the step, watching until the tail-lights had vanished, and Mariella had to say his name twice before he answered.

Singing at the villa had been a strain, but Julie was glad to have done it. It made a useful dress rehearsal for the club. Now she knew that she could stand up in front of Rico and sing songs of love and longing without breaking down.

On opening night, she sat in her dressing-room, applying her make-up. Gina, the elderly dresser, had told her that La Dolce Notte was filled to overflowing.

'You are so beautiful,' she said, standing back to admire. 'Not many women can wear such a dress.'

It was black satin with rows of sparkling beads around the hem. The cut was very tight, but Julie had the perfect figure to get away with its daring lines.

Gina excitedly ran through the names she'd spotted at the best tables. There were some show business celebrities and several prominent politicians.

'Guess who's sitting at Signor Rico's table? Salvatore Barono.'

Julie was startled at the name of the internationally famous Italian film star. He'd enjoyed a lucrative career in Hollywood, playing smooth Italian lovers, but he made occasional trips to his villa just outside Rome. These were always followed by press interviews about his need to return to 'the simple country pleasures'.

Rumour had it that behind the villa walls his pleasures were more scandalous than simple.

'What about Mariella?' Julie asked.

'She's here. She made sure she sat next to Signor Barono. Oh, *scusi, signore.*'

Rico had entered silently. He gave Gina a brief nod and she scuttled away. He didn't speak, but his eyes met Julie's in the mirror. She was startled. She hadn't seen him since the evening at the villa, and the sight came as a shock.

He was full of tension. His face was pale except for the dark shadows under his eyes, and there was a curious withered look about his mouth, as though he'd finally resigned himself to something unbearable.

'Are you all right?' he asked, and she heard in his voice the faint huskiness that meant he was sleeping badly.

'I'm fine. Did you come to see if I was wearing your diamonds? Don't worry. I know my duty.' She indicated the box on the dressing-table.

'Allow me.' She sat still while he draped the heavy jewels about her neck. 'They look splendid on you,' he said. 'In fact, your whole appearance is perfect.'

Once she'd sung in jeans and sweater and he'd whispered, 'I am jealous of every man who looks at you. You must be beautiful only for me.'

And she had answered, 'I don't see the others. Only you exist.'

But that was then. 'I'm glad I meet with your approval,' she said now.

'Are you nervous?'

'A little. That's good, though. It makes me perform better.'

'Anything for the performance,' he said wryly.

'Well, that's what I am. A performer. But after all, Rico, so are you. We just have to play the comedy out to the end.'

'I wonder what the end will be?'

'I'll complete my engagement, we'll shake hands and never see each other again. You'll probably marry Mariella. I wish you every happiness.'

'Shut up!' he said with soft violence. 'Do you think it hclps to talk likc that?'

She rose and faced him. 'What would help, Rico? I wish I knew, because somehow we have to get through the next three months. Ever since I came to Rome, we've done nothing but hurt each other. Let's keep well apart from now on.'

'It didn't have to be like that.'

'Perhaps it did. I don't think you could have stopped yourself from setting spies on me. It comes naturally to you to mistrust people. You can't stop now.' She saw him flinch as though her words were knives. In a gentler voice, she added, 'We had so much happiness once that I think we used it all up. Now we're getting all the pain in one go.'

'In one go?' he echoed bitterly. 'What about the past eight—' He stopped sharply.

So he, too, had lain awake in anguish, cursing the darkness but cursing the dawn still more because there was another day to be struggled through. And no baby caresses to sweeten his life.

Rico ran his hand through his hair in a gesture that was almost despairing. 'I wish I could say how I feel.'

'I think I know,' she said with a sigh. 'A little love, a lot of hate. And the hate is too strong for anything else to live in its shadow.'

His face hardened. 'Do you realize that you've just described your own feelings?'

She was about to say that she could never hate him. If her love didn't still burn brightly, he couldn't hurt her as he did. But she stopped herself. Rico was too dangerously strong. She must stay on her guard.

'Well, maybe you're right,' she said at last.

A light went out of his eyes. 'As long as we both know.' Then his manner became formal. 'Please accept my best wishes for your opening night. La Dolce Notte is very proud to have you as its star.' He gave her a curt, formal bow and departed.

She sat listening over the intercom as the orchestra struck up and the cabaret began. First a troop of dancers, then Beppe, singing the old songs, followed by a comedian. And finally...

'Ladies and gentlemen, we are proud to present that international singing sensation, Julie Hallam!'

She'd moved to the side of the stage, breathing slowly as she waited, concentrating every fibre of her being on the forthcoming performance. When she heard her name announced on a note of triumph, she burst onto the stage, smiling into the dazzling lights, acknowledging the applause with a wave, then storming into the first song before the applause had died.

She'd picked a razzle-dazzle opener that showed off her wide vocal range. It had no emotional depth, but the pyrotechnics grabbed her audience's attention and served notice that she had some surprises to spring. When she finished, the applause was loud and had the 'edge' that she always listened for. That edge was the first sign things were going well.

Having captured their attention, she segued into a dreamy ballad, and they listened eagerly, falling willingly under the spell she cast. She followed this with a song that was smoochy but with a hint of humour. Her eyes glinted with fun while her voice caressed the notes, offering her audience an experience that was both erotic and light-hearted. They responded with delight, and this time the applause had the full body that meant they were settling back to enjoy themselves.

After the third song, the lights came up for a few minutes to allow latecomers to get to their tables. Julie used this time chatting to the audience in the Italian she'd perfected. She enjoyed doing this as it gave her a chance to see their faces and establish a closer rapport. Tonight someone cried, '*Bellissima*!'

Laughing, Julie acknowledged the tribute with a little wave. '*Grazie, signore.*'

Once, little Patsy Brown had dreamed of commanding an audience in just this way. Now it was all coming true. Power streamed from her, the power of an artist at her peak, and she gloried in it.

She didn't need to look at Rico to be aware of him. She knew that he was sitting quite still, with an arrested quality to the angle of his head. And as if she'd gained second sight, she knew that she'd taken him by surprise.

He'd last seen her singing in the pub, little more than a raw amateur. Now she was a poised *chanteuse* who could hold an audience in the palm of her hand and do what she liked with it. He was watching her with eyes that feared to lose a moment, while Mariella, forgotten, sat beside him.

The starlet regarded him with narrowed eyes before turning a megawatt smile onto Salvatore Barono be-

side her. He returned it with some wattage to spare.
They were two of a kind.

The lights dimmed again and Julie got seriously to
work on her audience, teasing them, surprising them
whenever they thought they had her measure, beguil-
ing them with enchantment.

Then she grew very still, waiting for perfect silence.
In a slow, husky voice, she began to sing the song that
held a special meaning for one man.

> *'Whatever happened to my heart?*
> *I tried to keep it safe,*
> *But you broke through*
> *And stole it right away.*
> *Take good care of it,*
> *I'll never have another heart to give.'*

Tonight her voice had a passionate, edgy intensity
that had never been there before. And he had done
this, reviving turbulent emotions, giving her new depth
as a singer and as a woman. Suddenly the sophisticated club was alive with raw emotion. The fleeting
joys of first love, the aching knowledge of 'might have
been' and 'too late'. These worldly people had forgotten such feelings, but she made them remember and
fall silent.

Rico was shattered. She seemed to play with him at
will, haunting him with the past while showing him
how irrevocably the past was gone. It was like a phys-
ical pain, and he clenched his hands. He was shocked
at his own weakness. She was his enemy, yet she
could make him forget everything except how badly
he still wanted to possess her. Anger burned in him,
directed at himself as much as at her.

Julie had worked on her voice, extending her range so that she could stream up to an impossibly high and thrilling note. She saved it for the last song and gave it everything she had. Her performance brought the audience to their feet, clapping and cheering for so long that it seemed they would never let her go.

Before she could leave the stage, Rico rose and stretched out his hand, silently commanding her to take it. She did so.

'I promised you all the best,' Rico declared to everyone as the lights came up. 'And I delivered.' He kissed Julie's hand theatrically. 'You were wonderful!'

He snapped his fingers and a waiter handed him a single rose. It was dark crimson, velvety and perfect. Before the cheering crowd, he kissed it and presented it to Julie. She took it with a smile that matched his own, but she could see his eyes, and they were bleak.

He led her to his table and gestured for her to sit beside him. At once, Salvatore Barono leaned over and blasted her with brandy fumes.

'Eh, Rico! Introduce me to your little friend.'

He was older than he seemed on screen and had an unhealthy, raddled appearance. Julie greeted him politely but refused his invitation to sit beside him. And she had to fight not to back away from his drink-sodden breath.

The orchestra struck up for dancing, and the lights dimmed again, just enough for couples to be intimate in privacy. Barono flung out a hand towards Julie. 'We dance!' he announced, so melodramatically that she had to suppress a giggle.

'Please excuse me,' she said quietly but firmly. 'I'm a little tired after the performance.'

'A magnificent performance,' he declared. 'I wait

until the goddess is rested.' Turning to Mariella, he flung out his hand again and cried, 'We dance!' in exactly the same tone.

Concealing her chagrin at being so obviously second-best, Mariella took his hand. Together they smooched around the floor, each giving an exaggerated impression of being absorbed in the other. Julie placed her fingers tactfully over her mouth.

'He paid you a great compliment,' Rico observed. 'How unkind of you to laugh at him.'

'I can't help it. He's such a ham. And so is she.'

'You were superb tonight,' he said. 'Beyond my wildest dreams.'

'But you took a risk,' she reminded him. 'It wasn't my talent that made you bring me here. I might have disappointed you.'

'I knew your *singing* wouldn't disappoint me,' he said, emphasizing the word slightly. 'As for the rest, yes, I'd forgotten your stubbornness.'

'Eh, Rico, you did it again!'

A big man with a red face sat down at the table, bawling his appreciation. Rico winced and introduced him to Julie. She smiled and said the right things, and after a while he departed. His place was immediately taken by another man out of the same mould. He paid her fulsome compliments that she accepted with practised charm. Neither man could have guessed how she longed to be rid of them.

'Are you still angry with me?' Rico asked when they were alone again.

'No, only with myself. You warned me you'd try any trick to get the better of me. I should have listened. But I know now.'

'What do you think you know?'

'Everything about you that I'd rather not have known. You belong in this place. It's cold and obsessed with money and power, and you fit perfectly. I wish I'd never met you again.'

'Shut up!' he said with repressed fury. 'You don't know what you're talking about. You know nothing about me. And this place is your setting, too, don't forget. This is where you always wanted to be.'

'For my work, not my life,' she replied defiantly.

She gave a small gasp as his hand tightened. He'd been clasping her fingers ever more tightly as they spoke, and her last words made him so tense that his grip became unbearable.

'I'm sorry,' he said, releasing her at once. 'I didn't realize—I hope I didn't hurt you.'

'My fingers will recover. And perhaps in the end my heart will recover, too.'

'Then you are fortunate,' he flung at her. 'Damn you for sitting there so coolly while you wreak havoc everywhere! And damn my own stupidity for seeing in you anything but a heartless schemer. The sooner this farce is over, the better.'

'Rico!' A hot, damp hand grasped Julie's arm. Salvatore Barono had returned, his voice booming at them over the music. 'Wonderful evening! Wonderful singer! What a star!' His hand was inching its way round her waist.

'Thank you, you're too kind,' Julie murmured, trying to free herself from him.

'Don't be a dog in the manger, Rico,' the film star shouted, refusing to be dislodged. 'It's my turn to dance with the lady.'

'But you already have a partner,' Julie reminded him, indicating Mariella, who was looking furious.

'Oh, she'd rather dance with Rico,' Barono said blithely. 'And I'd rather dance with you. Come on, Rico, don't be greedy. It's time to share your toys.'

Julie's temper rose at this way of referring to her. She waited for Rico to drive the man away, but to her horror he made a gesture for her to accede.

'Rico,' she said urgently.

'You don't object to dancing with my friend, surely?' he asked her.

'But—'

'We're all friends together on these occasions.'

Rico silenced further argument by rising and taking Mariella into his arms. Reluctantly Julie let herself be claimed by Barono. He danced smoochily, holding her close and looking deep into her eyes. Julie wasn't fooled by this. It was for the public. And sure enough, there were photographers in place to record the moment.

'*Signorina*, you are very beautiful,' the actor said throatily.

'Really, you shouldn't—'

'But no, I speak only the truth. You are a radiant star in the firmament. What a couple we will make—'

'We aren't a couple,' she protested, trying to put some space between them.

He tightened his hand against the small of her back, drawing her close again. 'But we will be, we must...'

She turned her head, trying to avoid the booze fumes. But nothing could stop him. How could Rico subject her to this? she thought angrily. However much he hated her.

'We will go everywhere, and together we will make beautiful music.'

She couldn't believe he'd actually said that. Surely

nobody talked that way any more? Despite her annoyance, her lips twitched.

'You're teasing me,' he said. 'That means you secretly want me to make love to you—'

'It means no such thing,' she insisted, beginning to struggle in earnest. 'Let me go at once.'

'When we make love, you'll never want me to let you go.'

'We aren't going to make love—'

'I'm on fire for you. I can't wait.'

He tried to fix his mouth on hers, but she twisted aside. Instead he kissed her neck, sliding his lips down its length to the base of her throat. Julie wrenched her hands free and tried to thrust him away, but he was like a snake, insinuating himself everywhere. She felt as though she were struggling in a nightmare.

Then, suddenly, there was no need to struggle. Flashbulbs blinded her. Somewhere in the background, a woman screamed. There was a loud commotion. Barono slithered out of sight.

Rico had knocked him to the ground.

CHAPTER EIGHT

IN THAT second, something snapped inside Julie. As she saw Barono land on the floor with Rico standing over him, looking murderous, she fled blindly, not caring where she was going but plunging out through the audience.

She heard Rico call her name, but she didn't look back. She had to get away from here, away from him. For ever.

In a few moments, she was up the stairs and at the club entrance. Startled, people stared at her tear-stained face and distraught eyes, but nobody dared to stop her.

Then she was out in the street, running down the Via Veneto as fast as the tight dress would allow her. All about her were curious glances, but she ignored them and kept on. Safety was only a short distance away. The next side-street. She stumbled round the corner.

But everywhere was strange. It wasn't the right street. She looked frantically hither and thither, realizing that she was lost.

She turned back into the Via Veneto. She thought of the picture she presented, wearing a glamorous evening dress with no bag, no escort. The glances became leers and, horrified, she guessed what people must be thinking about her.

She tried to pull herself together. She must have turned the wrong way. It was just a question of retracing her steps. But that meant going past the club, and she wasn't sure she could do it.

Then a car screeched to a halt beside her. The driver uttered an oath as he saw her state, then leaped out. 'Get in,' Rico said.

'*I'm not going back there.*'

'No, I'll take you to the hotel. Get in.'

She looked at him wild-eyed, but she was too drained to resist. Gently but firmly he urged her into the car and drove in silence for the short distance. To her relief, he didn't go to the entrance but swung the car round the back and into an underground car park. From here the elevator ensured that they reached her suite undetected.

'My key,' she groaned. 'It's downstairs.'

Rico lifted a house phone on the wall and barked something into it. A moment later, someone came up in the main elevator with the key. Rico took it and opened her door. She slipped inside and tried to shut it in his face, but he wouldn't be refused.

Julie didn't even bother to switch on a lamp. The shutters were open and some of the glittering, multi-coloured lights from the street lit up the room in some places, throwing strange shadows in others. Julie began to strip off the jewellery, tossing it down without even looking where it fell.

'Have every last piece back.' she told him desperately. 'I can't stand any more. I'm getting the next plane out of here.'

'Julie, stop this, please. Listen—'

'No, you listen. I'm finished. And don't tell me I have a contract because the contract wasn't for any of the things you've made happen. You can sue me. I don't care if I ever work again. I don't need bright lights and fame. I just need…' She only needed Gary, but she checked herself on the brink of a dangerous revelation. 'I just need a quiet life,' she finished hurriedly.

As she spoke, she was tearing at a bracelet, but her shaking fingers couldn't undo the intricate clasp. At last she gave up and turned away from him, leaning against the wall and trembling with shock.

'Don't come near me,' she warned him in a fierce voice.

'Please, I only want to comfort you.'

'There's no comfort to be found in you, only tricks and heartless pretences.'

'You call *me* heartless?'

'What else should I call you? Everything about you is cold, heartless and merciless. There's nothing inside you any more, Rico, and that's what you can't bear, isn't it? Emptiness. A hollow where your heart should be. I'm sorry for you, and I'm sorry if it's my fault. Perhaps it is. Perhaps I did everything wrong all those years ago, but I was only seventeen. What did I know about anything?'

'Julie—'

'*Don't touch me*! Don't ever try to touch me again. Go back to Mariella and the others. They're all you're good for.'

His face darkened. 'Would you condemn me to that?'

'You condemned yourself a long time ago. Stick to them. Use them as they use you. Sleep with them. Tell them all the lies they want to hear, then pay them off. That's the language they understand. But don't confuse me with them. How—how could you make such an exhibition of me?'

'Of myself, surely,' he said harshly. 'Now the world knows that I can't endure you to be touched by another man. Do you think I wanted that?'

'You forced me to dance with him.'

'Because I was mad with rage and pride. How else could I be when you—'

'Stop it! I don't want to know. I'm taking the first plane out. Don't try to stop me. Don't follow me. For pity's sake, Rico, let this be the end!'

Now he would vow to watch her for ever until he found their son. But instead of threats, he spoke the very last words she had expected in a quiet, melancholy voice. 'You mean to abandon me yet again?'

'You manage very well without me,' she said huskily. 'Go back to your money and your mistresses.'

'Only one woman has ever been mistress of my heart,' he said in the same quiet voice, as though he was discovering the truth only as he spoke it. 'Once, I needed you very much. You'll never know how much. You left me stranded in a frozen nothingness and now you can't bear what I've become, so you're going to desert me again. You've called me many names tonight, Julie. I wonder how you'll like the one I call you. Coward.'

She stared at him, shocked by the accusation.

'Maybe I'm all that you say,' he went on. 'Cruel, treacherous, untrustworthy, and many more things you don't dream of. I seek bad company because that's where I'm most at ease. But you, more than anyone in the world, know that I once was a better man.

'Perhaps you're right to go. Nobody will try to follow you. My word on it. As soon as you've gone from here, you'll also be gone from my life, and I will wipe you out of my heart.'

It was the worst threat he could have uttered. To exist for him no more!

'I'll make sure you're left in peace,' he said. Then he gave a short, mirthless laugh. 'Peace. For us. Is there such a thing?'

'Rico…'

He stopped at something new in her voice. He didn't look at her, but he grew very still as though trying to believe what he'd heard.

'*Rico*…'

He moved fast, and the next moment he'd seized her up into his arms. She reached out, clinging to him desperately, crying his name in a choking voice.

'Don't leave me,' he said. 'I won't let you.'

'How can I stay? How can I go?'

'I didn't mean it to happen like that tonight. I went mad watching you—I thought I could stand it but—kiss me, *kiss me*—'

He smothered her mouth like a man at the limit of endurance. His lips were hard and purposeful, just as she'd always loved them. Before she knew it, her arms were about his neck, and she was obeying his order to kiss him—obeying it again and again. She'd never loved him as much as now when his need and desolation were spread before her.

'I could have killed him,' he grated. 'How dare he touch you!'

'You wanted him to—'

'*Like hell I did*!'

Her head was spinning. She was sure there were things they ought to say first, but she couldn't remember them. The terrible words they'd hurled at each other vanished into the past. The passion of his kisses blotted out all memory of his actions.

'Rico—'

'No,' he said firmly. 'No more words. It's with words that we hurt each other.'

He kissed her again before she could answer. She sensed that he was quickly losing control, and the knowledge thrilled her. Her own control was slipping fast. Over the years, she'd suppressed all desire until she'd almost forgotten how it felt. But with Rico the years vanished. Desire still burned with a steady flame, ready to leap up to new heights, as it was doing now.

But even as it flared, she felt Rico put a brake on himself. He fixed his hands on her shoulders and drew back, gasping.

'What's wrong?' she asked, bewildered.

'Tell me that you're sure,' he said urgently.

'I'm sure. Truly.'

'We've made so many mistakes. If this isn't what you really want—'

'There's nothing I want more than this. Don't say any more. You said it yourself. We don't need words.'

Nothing could have held him after that. Quickly he removed her dress, pulling the long zip down her back so that the satin slid down with a whisper. It seemed as though her sophisticated persona fell away with it, and she again became a trusting girl, blindly following her heart into the arms of the boy she adored.

'Tell me that you want me,' he murmured. 'Promise me that it's true.'

He was kissing her between words, enticing her with his lips, sending flickers of feeling along her ragged nerves. She tried to think, but he was purposely denying her the chance, invoking her desire. Julie clung to him, longing for the strength to break away and longing, too, to stay in his arms for ever.

'I want you,' she whispered in answer as he drew her to the bed and lay down with her. 'I've always wanted you…all these years—'

'Hush,' he said against her mouth. 'The years have never been. We met today, and there is no tomorrow….'

He smelled of spice and earth, of sun and wind and desire. His skin was hot with passion yet smooth as marble, his frame lean, muscular and powerful. He was the man who had brought her flesh to life long ago, in another life. It had vibrated to him alone. Now it lived again under his touch.

There was skill in his fingers. They knew how to give feather-light caresses that she barely felt, except that they increased the fires raging inside her. He traced the length of her, the beautiful swell of her breasts, her tiny waist and the womanly curve of her hips, and with every touch, he reclaimed her.

Julie gave herself up to him as simply as she had done the first time, without fear or reservation. And he was everything she'd hoped—passionate but tender, loving her with care. He evoked her desire slowly, seeking to please her, savouring the miracle that had been given back to them. When their moment came, he asked again, 'Do you really want me?' as though he were afraid of the answer. She gave him the answer he wanted with her mouth, with her body and with her whole soul.

After so long apart, they were like strangers, yet strangers who knew each other mysteriously well. Over the years, he'd gained in skill and control, but his ardour was the same, as was the reverence with which he touched her body.

Their union was heart-stopping in its beauty. She

had forgotten that such pleasure existed, but great as it was, it was still less than the flowering of love. How had she lived so long without him? How could she bear to be without him ever again?

'*My love*,' she whispered. '*My love…*'

'Tell me that you forgive me,' he said as they lay quietly together, wrapped in each other's arms. 'Say it, for I need to hear it very much.'

'I forgive you,' she murmured against his skin.

She regarded him with wonder, awed by what had just happened. The lights from the street that never slept flickered over his body in a myriad of colours. In the shadows, there were no details, only the magnificent outline of a male body in its prime. She had left a boy. She found a man.

'What are you thinking?' he murmured.

'I'm not thinking,' she said with a little smile. 'Who wants to think when they can feel like this? Are you thinking?'

He shook his head and gave the laugh of a man who had just conquered the world and found it lovely. It did her heart good to hear him.

'Yet perhaps I should be thinking,' he mused. 'I've done so many clumsy things to offend you.' He saw a shadow cross her face. 'About the other night—I'm not as guilty as you think me. It's true that I had you watched as soon as you arrived in Rome—'

'And that evening?'

'Yes, that evening. It began as you thought, a way of persuading you. But that's not how it ended. You sent that old horse home, and I remembered the dog and how you could never bear any creature to be hurt. Then I knew that you were still Patsy.'

'No,' she said quickly.

'Why won't you let me call you Patsy?'

'Because she belongs to the past, and the past is over. The love we had then was beautiful, but we can't have it back. We can only build on the present and make a new love from the people we are now.'

'Can we do that?'

'I don't know. We can try.'

'How wise you are. Then are you wise enough to understand that that night I forgot everything except the happiness of being with you? I even forgot the men who were watching us or I'd have called them off. I swear I would.'

He made a grimace of self-mockery. 'If you wanted to punish me, you succeeded. I was a laughing-stock, both at the fountain and in the hotel. Rico Forza, stood up like a ninny, hammering uselessly at a woman's door.'

'I was just too unhappy to think straight. I wasn't trying to punish you, Rico.'

'I know that now.' He smiled wryly. 'I just thought you might enjoy the joke.'

'And Mariella? Is she a joke?'

'Mariella and I have what is practically a business relationship. We show each other off for the paparazzi. But after tonight she won't waste her time with me. Barono will suit her better, and he's welcome. I've been lashing out, hurting you and myself, not knowing why I did so. But I know now, *mio amore*. It's because I—'

'Hush,' she said urgently. 'Don't say it unless you're sure.'

'You think I'm not sure? Why have I been unable to love any woman but you, years after I should have forgotten you? And you? Whom have you loved? No, don't tell me.' His finger was quickly across her mouth. 'I don't want to know. It's enough that you are in my arms now.'

She understood. The shoals that threatened them still lay underneath. There was so much they didn't dare talk about. But like him, she wanted to forget the problems and think only of the beauty. And there was so much beauty.

He enfolded her in his arms again and they loved away the night. She was dazed with delight and a touch of disbelief that everything had been given back to her so completely.

Too good to be true.

That phrase had rung in her head before, and she'd found it disastrously true. But not now. This time, she had to believe in him because the lover who adored her so reverently could only be true to her. On that thought she fell into a peaceful sleep.

Rico found that if he only opened his eyes halfway, he could see the dawn but not the details of the room. In that way, it was possible to believe that time had moved back eight years, and he was once again in a shabby room in London. The girl he loved was nestled against him, softly breathing in the satiety of love. His arms curved about her protectively as well as possessively. They were young and in love, and the world belonged to them.

Then he opened his eyes fully. The room came jarring back into place, and he groaned at how easily he'd been seduced by a memory. He'd sworn never to forget the injury this woman had done him, yet he'd forgotten it with the first kiss. How willingly he'd let her take him back to their golden days, days that could never be recovered except in dreams.

He recalled his own passionate, loving words—words he'd used to no other woman but her. What a fool he'd been! A blind, besotted, sentimental fool, to let her know how easily she could conquer him! His pride revolted at the thought of how she would laugh.

He moved slightly, and it disturbed her. She rolled onto her back so that her head was turned towards him and he could see her face. It was pale in the morning light and oddly defenceless. He could see shadows beneath her eyes, and even in sleep there was a look of strain about her mouth, as though she knew of some burden that would weigh her down the moment she awoke.

Despite his angry thoughts, he could feel himself softening towards her. Her tousled hair made her look younger, vulnerable, and the old tenderness began to warm him again. How often had he longed to gather her up in his arms, hide her away where the world could never find her and take her to a place where they could live only for each other?

But no such place existed. There was only the harsh world of buying and selling, cheating and lying, winning and losing. Who knew that better than he did? And who but she had taught him?

He thought of the damage he'd done to himself last night, the film deal with Barono that would fall through now, the lawsuit that would cost him a fortune. And all because the sight of her being pawed by that slimy lecher had been too much to swallow. He'd forced her into Barono's arms as a gesture of power, and that action had rebounded on him, as everything about this woman did.

He eased himself quietly out of bed, then dressed quickly. Shame scalded him at how easily he'd become her dupe again. She mustn't suspect. He could better live with his weakness if it were known only to himself.

He let himself quietly out into the corridor. His last view was of Julie sleeping like a baby, her arm flung out to the place where he ought to have been. It made him feel like a murderer, but he didn't stop. He was like a man escaping with his life.

It was dawn and the streets were almost empty as he drove, not to his villa, but to a small room in the unfashionable part of the city, which he used when he needed to shake off the shiny trappings of his life and be himself alone. He kept his mind deliberately empty to avoid brooding on the way he'd abandoned her within hours of the most tender loving they'd ever known. If he didn't think about it, he might feel less of a murderer.

But he'd chosen the wrong place for shutting her out. This was where he kept his mementoes of her. There weren't many, just the things he'd taken with him on his trip to Italy. A scarf he'd bought her, which had still borne the fresh, flowery perfume she used; a picture to show his grandfather.

'Look, Grandfather, how pretty she is!'

'You're very lucky, my boy.'

The old man's smiling face. And all the time, *smash, smash* behind his back. Until there was nothing left of love, or hope, or youth.

She'd trusted him totally. Her face, as she saw him off, had been without fear.

And how had he repaid her trust?

The scarf and the photograph were in his hands

now. He'd thrust them into the back of a drawer, telling himself that one day soon he would destroy them. But one day had never come.

Her face was heartbreakingly young, looking back at him from the picture. '*I was only seventeen. What did I know about anything?*'

He threw off his clothes and showered, trying to find peace and a feeling of cleanliness. But both had deserted him. He recalled his anger, hoping it would justify his behaviour to himself. But all that would come into his mind was the memory of Julie lying in his arms, her face aglow with joy, whispering, 'My love…my love…'

He could see her now, waking up, smiling and reaching for him, finding him gone.

The thought of her face when she discovered his desertion almost made him weaken. There was still time to put it right. A bouquet of red roses with a note making some excuse for his early departure, asking to see her this morning…

He found he was forming the words in his head. He reached out a hand to call the florist.

Then he froze.

This woman could make him weak as no other woman could, and weakness was a sin that he'd abjured years ago. He must fight her even if it meant fighting his own softer nature. To do that, he needed to get away. He wasn't safe in the same city, the same country. He should call, not the florist, but the airport.

But never to hold her in his arms again, never to hear her voice whispering his name out of the depths of passion, never to see her eyes shining with love.

For a long moment, he stayed as he was, tortured by indecision.

Then he lifted the receiver…

CHAPTER NINE

WHEN she opened her eyes, Julie knew she would find Rico looking down at her tenderly, as so often in the past. She was so convinced of this that she delayed the pleasure, lying still and listening for the sound of his breathing. When she couldn't hear it, she gave a puzzled little frown and opened her eyes.

She was alone in the bed. Only the rumpled sheets on the other side showed that Rico had ever been there. There was no sign of him.

Perhaps he was having a shower. But the bathroom was empty. Rico was nowhere to be seen. His clothes, too, had vanished.

It was seven in the morning. He had risen at the crack of dawn, dressed quietly and slipped away without a word, without leaving behind him even so much as a short note.

Julie stood in the centre of the floor, looking slowly about her, trying to take in the fact that she had been abandoned. A chill seemed to start deep down and rise until it enclosed her heart.

The memory of his love was still in her flesh. Last night she'd lain in his arms, listening to his impassioned words. And this morning he was gone. Surely he would call at any moment to say he'd had to rush home because he was expecting a vital phone call.

She breakfasted in her room, waiting. But there was no call.

Finally she could deny the truth no longer. His disappearance was a cold snub. He'd gained what he wanted, then vanished without a backward glance.

On the first evening, he'd said, 'I've paid for you. And what I've paid for, I will take.'

And now he'd taken it. Or rather, he'd beguiled her into offering it freely. This was his revenge for her refusal to tell him about their son.

She lifted her head and told herself that she didn't care. To give herself something to do, she went sight-seeing around Rome, trying to believe that she was interested in the ancient monuments. Afterwards she couldn't remember where she'd been.

She returned to the hotel to find that there were no messages for her. She walked to the club, wondering if Rico would be there, what he would say to her, how he would look.

But instead she met Galena, his secretary, about to leave, looking ruffled.

'Why does he dump these last-minute decisions onto me?' she demanded. 'He never said anything about New York before, but all of a sudden he has to be there today. First flight out. Everything done in a rush.'

'New York?' Julie echoed, stunned. 'He's gone?'

'This morning. Just like that. I don't know what the crisis is, and he didn't tell me. I've been on the phone all day changing his appointments.'

'You mean…rescheduling them for when he re-turns?' Julie said, trying not to sound as though her heart was hammering.

'I don't know when he's coming back,' Galena said bitterly.

'But…surely he won't be away for long?'

Galena looked at her shrewdly, and Julie suddenly

saw herself through the secretary's eyes: another of Rico Forza's women who'd served her purpose and been shrugged aside. There was even a hint of sympathy in the older woman's eyes that made Julie's cheeks flame.

'Maybe he isn't coming back,' Galena said. 'He has an apartment over there, and the last time he went, he stayed for over three months.'

Three months. By that time, she would have left Rome. It was a slap in the face.

She seemed to perform on automatic that night, but the audience noticed nothing wrong. They cheered her enthusiastically. She was still in a state of shock when she returned to the hotel.

She went out early next morning. She didn't know where she was going, but she had to get away. She found a small car-hire firm just opening, asked for a convertible and drove off.

Her driving was steady, but her mind seethed. Rico had snubbed her cruelly, and he'd done it after a night when their souls had seemed as close as their bodies. She could almost feel her heart breaking in her breast, but she refused to feel it. Nor would she let herself cry. She'd wept enough tears for Rico. The time for weeping was over.

Soon she began to smell salty air. She'd travelled barely fifteen miles when the glittering sea came into view, and she slowed down to look at the most beautiful shoreline she had ever seen.

It had a long stretch of fine golden sand, edged by a small forest of sea pines. Villas and bungalows were dotted about under the trees, and from them issued bathers, clutching towels, which they spread out on the sand.

What a delightful spot this would be for a vacation, she thought. The beach was clean and well equipped, but not crowded. How Gary would have loved it here!

She kicked off her shoes and began to stroll along the water's edge. This magic place made such a blessed contrast to the world she'd escaped, a world of jagged nerves, tortured feelings and betrayal.

She had the strangest sensation, as though a tunnel had opened up in her mind. Looking back through it, she could see that the signs had been there all along. Rico had never quite been convincing as a poor boy. That touch of imperiousness had always been there, ready to flash out without warning. The arrogance of the Caesars had been born in him, and only her ignorance had prevented her seeing it.

He'd been a stranger in her country. She'd had all the advantages, but despite this, he'd led, she'd followed. It seemed natural. She remembered how he sometimes instinctively gave orders. She would make fun of him, saying demurely, '*Sì, signore.*' And he would redden and quickly add, 'Please.'

She tried not to let her mind dwell on the night they'd shared, which already seemed a million years ago. His tenderness and ardour had moved her to tears, and she'd dared to hope that she'd touched his heart again. And all the time his cold pride had been rejecting her.

Some part of her life had ended. She wept for him more than for herself. Over the years, everything had been taken from him, his young passion, his child, the generous nature that had made him so lovable. Now he'd lost the last thing of all—her love. And he'd lost it because it no longer meant anything to him.

Standing by the water, looking out over the sea, she made the saddest resolution of her life.

I will love him no more.

It would be hard and terrible, for loving him had been her pride and joy. But she couldn't afford to love the man he had become. She'd fought Arturo Forza for Rico's soul. And she'd lost.

She found a coffee-shop on the edge of the beach. It was already busy and she had to share a table with a cheerful family. They were happy to tell their business to the whole world, and soon she knew how long they'd been in this little resort, which was called Fregene, when they were going home and how much they'd paid for their villa.

'Lovely place for kids,' the father said. 'Right on the beach, smashing weather. Plenty to do. You got kids?'

She told them about Gary, and as she talked, her longing for him grew. It seemed an age since she'd seen him. As soon as she could, she escaped and put through a call to Aunt Cassie.

'Thank goodness I caught you,' she said. 'I was afraid you might have gone out.'

'No chance of that,' Cassie said. 'It's raining cats and dogs for the past four days. Gary's being very good, but the poor little soul is bored stiff. Here he is.'

The sound of her son's voice brought an ache to Julie's heart.

'Hallo, Mommy. Are you having a nice time?'

'It's not a holiday, precious. I'm working.'

'I know. But I wish you didn't have to go away to work.'

'I'll never go away from you again,' she vowed. 'After this, we're going to stick together.'

'I miss you, Mommy.'

'I miss you, too, darling.'

'When are you coming home?'

'It'll be a while yet. I—oh, darling, please don't cry.'

'I'm not crying, Mommy,' he said, trying to sound firm, although she could hear his voice wobble.

Julie made a sudden decision. 'Would you like to come out here and see me?'

'Yes, please.' His eagerness thrilled her and demonstrated how badly he'd missed her more than his words ever could.

She talked to Cassie again and briefly outlined the inspiration that had just come to her. 'This place is only about fifteen miles from Rome. I can rent a villa on the beach for you and visit as often as possible.'

I'm crazy, she thought as she hung up. There might not even be any villas free. I don't even know how to hire one.

But luck was with her. Fregene was a small place and she found the agency hiring the villas without difficulty. There was one vacancy, a tiny bungalow, just big enough. Julie snapped it up with a sense of exultancy.

It seemed like fate to have all the pieces falling into place so easily. Only a little while earlier, she would never have dared bring Gary to Italy, so close to Rico, but her resolution to fight back had given her a feeling of power. Suddenly there was no problem she couldn't solve.

She called Cassie again, gave her the details and told her to take the next plane out. She was smiling as she went back to the car. In a day or two, she would embrace her darling little son again. She could hardly contain her excitement.

She took possession of the empty bungalow at once, then spent a rapturous day buying gifts for Gary to find there when he arrived. By that afternoon, she had several new sets of clothes, a bucket and spade, a beach ball and some colouring books. For Cassie, she bought a pure silk scarf and blouse.

Rico hadn't returned and there was no word from him. It looked as though his absence was going to be prolonged. Julie summoned up all her strength and behaved as normal, showing no reaction. She even booked Carlo for a rehearsal next morning as she wanted to make some changes in the act.

She removed some of the livelier numbers, replacing them with sad songs, which made Carlo's eyebrows rise. He said nothing directly, but when they'd finished and were having a drink in the bar, he observed casually, 'I gather there's no sign of Rico coming back yet.'

Julie shrugged.

'Don't,' Carlo said gently. 'Don't pretend you don't care. It doesn't suit you.'

'You've got it all wrong, Carlo. There's nothing between Rico and me.'

'Julie, *cara*, you're talking to a man who had a front-row view of Rico's face when he knocked Barono down. He was ready to do murder. Whatever there is or isn't on your side, there's plenty on his.'

'Then where is he?' Julie asked wretchedly. 'How could he just walk out on me after—'

'I know Rico. When there's something he can't cope with, he simply withdraws deep into himself. For

years now, he's lived by only allowing himself super-
ficial emotions. It's his defence. If something has
pierced it, then that's what he's most afraid of.

'It's lucky he didn't become a banker. He's got a
way of acting impulsively, then regretting it when it's
too late. But in the past, it's always been about things
that didn't matter too much. If he's found something
that matters…there's no knowing what he may do.'

Julie was at the airport with an hour to spare, agitated
in case the plane was delayed. But it was on time, and
there was Cassie and Gary waving at her. Gary came
flying into her arms, almost suffocating her with his
hug.

'Oh, darling,' she said passionately. 'How I've
missed you! Mmmm! Come here and let me squeeze
you again.'

They made a merry journey to Fregene. She showed
them over the villa, watched with delight as they
opened their presents, then let Gary drag her down the
beach to the sea. Cassie chose to stay behind and put
her feet up.

Gary was thrilled with the golden sands, the sea, the
delicious ice creams. They frolicked in the water,
splashing it over each other and screaming with laughter.

Seeing Gary in this setting, she could appreciate
how truly Rico's son he was, not merely because he
resembled his father, but because he looked Italian.
His black hair and large dark eyes belonged here. And
although he was only seven, there was already something in his proud carriage that proclaimed his heri-
tage. How delighted with him Rico would be! If only
that day might come soon!

She stayed as late as she dared, aching to remain with him. Luckily the day's excitement caught up with him all at once, and he fell asleep as soon as his head touched the pillow.

Julie sat beside him, stroking his hair. 'I'll be back soon,' she whispered.

In fact, she was able to return the next day and the one after. The time they spent together on the beach would have been blissful but for the aching of her heart. She wondered if she would ever see Rico again.

He arrived one night when she was in the middle of her act, and stood, unnoticed, at the back of the club.

Julie had discarded the glitzy dress she'd worn for the opening and chosen something floaty in grey silk chiffon, with pearls the only adornment. She'd varied her programme, too. Some of the dazzling numbers had gone to make room for the songs of loss and desolation. She sang these as she'd never sung before, with an aching intensity that hushed the room. Rico dropped his head, listening with a hand covering his eyes.

Afterwards he vanished without a word, and Julie might never have known he'd been there but for Carlo's murmuring, 'Rico was in tonight.'

Late as it was, she arrived home to find his bouquet of red roses with a card that said simply, 'R.' She wondered whom he hauled out of bed at this hour to provide them.

She heard a soft tap at her door. Julie drew in her breath sharply at the sight of the man who stood outside. Rico looked as if he hadn't slept for a week. His face was ravaged and his eyes burned. He didn't speak but stood looking at her in silence until at last she stood back to let him in.

'You were wonderful tonight,' he said jerkily. 'As always.'

'Did you come here to discuss my performance?'

'No, I came to apologize. I know what you must think of me—going away like that. It wasn't…what you thought.'

'How do you know what I thought?' she asked quietly.

'I didn't just walk out on you—'

'But you did.'

'I didn't mean it like that,' he said roughly. 'I always meant to come back—no, that's not true. At first I never meant to come back. Do you mind if I sit down?'

The question burst out abruptly, and she realized that he was on the verge of collapse. When she nodded, he sat down heavily on the bed and buried his face in his hands.

'You look as if you've only just got off the plane,' she said.

'No, I—' he checked his watch '—I flew back last night. I was going to come and see you today, but I walked about instead. At least, I think so. I can't really remember. I can't sleep on planes and my body clock is still several hours behind. I'm not making much sense, am I?'

'Enough to tell me that you're half-dead from jet lag. You shouldn't have come here tonight, Rico. Go home and get some sleep.'

'I couldn't go home without seeing you first. I don't seem to have much courage left, but I have just enough for that. Perhaps it was a mistake, though.'

She was about to tell him angrily that it was the biggest mistake he'd ever made, thinking he could simply walk back into her life after delivering such a blunt snub. But the words died in the face of his exhaustion and the despair written plainly on his face. If she'd had a bad time, so had he.

Instead she said, 'Thank you for the flowers.'

'I wanted to say something on the card, but I couldn't think of anything to say. I spent five days in New York wondering where I was going. In the end, I knew the only right way was back to you.'

'Don't say things like that,' Julie told him quickly.

'No, I don't suppose you're ready to hear them, are you?'

'No,' she said quietly. 'We have a long way to go, Rico, and perhaps we'll never get there. I've been able to do a lot of thinking while you were away. It would have been better if we'd never met again. Perhaps it would have been better if we'd never met in the first place.'

'Do you really mean that?' he asked, looking at her out of distraught eyes.

Never to have known his love, no matter how much pain followed? Even if she hadn't been blessed with her son, would she really have wanted that? Dumbly she shook her head.

'When did you have something to eat?' she asked.

He shrugged. 'I had a few drinks in the club.'

'That won't do you any good,' she said like a mother. 'You need some proper food inside you and something to drink that isn't alcohol.'

She called room service and ordered omelettes and tea. Rico didn't move, but his eyes never left her.

'Go over to the other side of the bed,' she said. 'Then the waiter won't see you from the door.'

He obeyed her like a child. A few minutes later, she answered the knock on the door. The waiter had a small table that he wheeled just inside, but Julie prevented him from coming any farther in and setting it up. She signed the bill, gave him a tip and closed the door behind him.

'You'll feel better when you've had some of this,' she said, wheeling the table directly into the room. 'I ordered mushroom omelettes because I remember you like them. Rico?'

There was no answer. Rico was stretched out on the bed, dead to the world.

She sat beside him and laid her hand against his face, feeling all bitterness and anger drain away. She didn't know what would happen between them now. She'd learned caution in a hard school and was far from sure that they could ever find a future together. But she couldn't maintain her hostility to this vulnerable man.

She'd told herself that the battle for his soul was over. She'd conceded defeat. Now she knew it wasn't over at all because Rico himself was still fighting to reclaim his better self. How could she abandon him to fight alone?

She left him to sleep and turned the lights down, leaving herself only enough to eat by. Then she undressed quietly and went to sleep on the sofa.

After a while, Rico began to toss and turn restlessly, muttering in his sleep. Julie lay down on the bed beside him, putting her arm over him protectively. After that, he was able to rest.

*   *   *

Julie awoke first and was having breakfast when Rico opened his eyes. After he stumbled into the bathroom, she heard the sound of a shower, followed by the electric shaver attached to the wall. When he emerged, he'd dressed again in the ruffled shirt and black trousers he'd worn to the club last night.

She poured him a coffee. He was nervous. His arrogance had fallen away from him and he was watching her closely, trying to determine her mood. She wondered how much he recalled about last night.

'I'm sorry for passing out like that,' he said.

'You were just about ready for it.'

'I always seem to be making apologies to you.'

'It's not important, Rico.'

'No, I suppose not,' he said, sounding disconcerted. He drank his coffee while wandering about the room. By the window, he discovered a pile of newspapers several days old.

'We made the front pages,' Julie said calmly. She was keeping her voice light and neutral, partly because she was feeling her way inch by inch, and partly because she didn't want to put any emotional pressure on him.

She had the strangest feeling that all the cards were now in her hands. She wasn't used to feeling this way with Rico, and it was taking her a while to come to terms with it. So she was playing her hand with great care, frightened of playing the wrong card or the right one at the wrong moment. Perhaps they had a chance. But only perhaps.

He seated himself and began studying the papers.

The headlines were stark.

Nightclub Owner Assaults Film Star.

Rico Forza Socks Barono In Jealousy Brawl.

There were several pictures, but the best one showed Rico standing over the supine Barono, who was rubbing his jaw and looking undignified. Julie stood there, looking horrified, while Mariella seemed at swooning point.

'I picked up a couple of papers yesterday,' Rico observed. 'Mariella has been giving interviews claiming that I assaulted Barono because I was jealous of the attentions he was paying her.'

'But he was dancing with me!'

'He'd been dancing with her a few minutes earlier. Apparently I'd been watching them, seething with rage and jealousy. I urged you to dance with him as a way of separating him from Mariella, but she used our dance to inform me that she'd transferred her affections, at which it seems that I was overcome by the strength of my feelings.'

'So why didn't you stay with her instead of rushing out after me?'

He shrugged. 'Anything for a good story. It doesn't have to make sense. I'm sorry to have exposed you to all this.'

'Don't worry. I got some lovely reviews. Look at page thirty-seven.'

It was a review any singer would die for. The critic had waxed lyrical about her technical skill and her deep emotional impact. Rico read it and grunted his satisfaction.

A terrible thought occurred to Julie. 'You didn't order them to write that, did you? You did. You've got shares in that paper.'

'No, I swear it. You earned this on your own merit. I'm glad for you, Julie. It's no more than you deserve.' He stirred his coffee. 'Where do we go from here?'

'I honestly don't know.'

'I wouldn't blame you for hating me.'

'I don't hate you, Rico,' she said earnestly. 'But loving you is too dangerous.'

'I suppose I asked for that.'

'I didn't mean—oh, dear.'

'We need time for a long talk. We'll spend the day together and—'

'Oh, Rico, I can't. I'm sorry.'

'I mean, will you please spend the day with me?' he corrected himself hastily.

'It's not that. It's just that I've made other plans.'

'Can't you break them?'

'No,' she said, thinking of Gary's face if she broke her word to come next day.

'What can you have planned that's more important than…? I'm sorry,' he quickly apologized.

'I could make it tomorrow,' she offered.

'Tomorrow it is, then.'

CHAPTER TEN

SHE knew she'd made the right decision as soon as she saw Gary next morning. They'd planned exactly how they would spend the day, and the little boy remembered every detail of every promise. It would have been terrible to let him down.

Both Gary and Cassie were crazy about boats, while Julie wasn't keen on sailing. So they set up a boat trip for the two of them the day after, and Julie was free to stay in Rome with Rico.

He came to her dressing-room that night as she was getting ready. She wasn't feeling very well, having spent too long in the sun. Now her head was aching, and she would have been glad of an early night. But her audience was waiting, expecting the best.

'Will you be all right?' Rico asked. 'You look tired.'

'I am,' she said, passing a hand over her eyes. 'But it makes no odds. I perform when I'm tired, when I'm sad, even—' her voice shook '—even when there seems nothing to hope for.'

'It's a sin to give up hope. Remember that.'

'Is it?' she asked with a little sigh. 'Then I must be a great sinner, for sometimes I—I don't think there's any point.'

'Julie, please...'

He made a movement towards her. She didn't know how she might have received it if they hadn't heard

Gina approaching in the corridor. Rico drew back as though stung, then hurried out of the room.

As she had hoped, as soon as she was in the spotlight, the adrenalin took over, and she sang her heart out. She couldn't see Rico, but she knew he was out there somewhere, listening to every word, every inflection of sadness and loss.

He didn't appear in her dressing-room afterwards, but she found him waiting outside, his back against the wall, staring at the floor, lost in thought. When she touched his arm, he looked up before his defences were in place. In his eyes she saw not just apprehension but the dreadful, sickening fear of a man who'd understood too late, when he'd already thrown the prize away.

He spoke as though roused from a dream. 'I'll drive you home.'

'I prefer to walk.'

'You can't walk home alone at this hour,' he said at once.

Was it an accident that he'd used words so close to the ones he'd spoken on that night long ago, the night when they'd found each other? His dark face made it hard to tell. But his next words settled it.

'Why does your lover permit such a thing?' he whispered.

She looked him in the eye. 'I don't have a lover. Only men who admire me, who want to own me or show me off. A lover is something different.'

He remembered. 'And you said that you wanted to be more than a trophy,' he reminded her.

'Yes, I said that. But a trophy is what I seem to have ended up.'

'Not to me,' he said quietly. He added with meaning, 'If you were mine, I wouldn't let you walk alone in the dark.'

'I'm not yours,' she told him. 'But you may walk me home.'

Together they strolled the three blocks along the Via Veneto, but at the corner of the street that led to her hotel, she stopped.

'We'll say good-night here.'

'I'll call you tomorrow?'

'Yes, but not too soon. I'd like to sleep late.'

'*Buona notte, signorina.*'

'*Buona notte,* Signor Forza.'

Next morning's papers were full of Barono and Mariella, who'd managed to get themselves featured every day since the incident in the nightclub. This time, they'd descended on the Via Condotti and raided every shop. Barono had loaded his new love with the costliest of everything, while ensuring that the camera didn't see too much of his black eye.

Julie read all this while eating a leisurely breakfast of rolls and coffee in bed.

The phone rang.

'I hope I didn't wake you,' Rico said.

'No, I was reading the papers. They've done it again, particularly in—' She named a Roman scandal sheet.

'I've been reading that, too. Perhaps we should give the press some pictures of our own, to make the true position clear. When may I call for you?'

'I'll be ready in an hour. And by the way, dress casually.'

'Where are we going?'

'I'll tell you when I see you.'

She was waiting for him downstairs, wearing de-
signer jeans and a blue silk shirt, roped in at the waist
by a multicoloured silk sash. A matching scarf kept
her hair back. Rico had obeyed her injunction and was
in shirtsleeves, with a fawn linen jacket slung over his
shoulder.

'Where to?' he asked.

'The zoo.'

'The zoo?'

'You promised me long ago.'

'The zoo it is, then.'

'Is it far?' she asked as they began to walk.

He pointed along the Via Veneto. 'No distance. At
the end of this street are the Borghese Gardens, and
the zoo is on the far side. We could take a *carrozza*
if we can find one.'

He looked around as he spoke, but it was Julie who
saw something that made her give a delighted squeal.

'Over there!' she said, clutching his arm and pointing to an elderly horse clip-clopping placidly down the
far side of the street. Behind him, the driver sat with
his head sunk on his chest. 'That's Miko, I'm sure of
it. Come on!'

'Julie, wait!' Rico roared, making a frantic grab for
her, just too late to stop her from darting out into traffic. An oncoming car braked just in time. The driver,
finding his engine stalled, stuck his head out and
shrieked Roman curses. Horns tooted, drivers bawled.
Rico raced across the wide road to where Julie had
halted Miko in his tracks by the simple expedient of
planting herself in front of him and seizing his bridle.
Miko's driver seemed to wake up.

'*Buon giorno, signorina,*' he called cheerfully.
'Miko is very happy to see you again. And so am I.'

'Get in,' Rico said, grabbing her arm and shoving her unceremoniously into the *carrozza*.

'Hey—'

'Get in before you cause a riot, you madwoman. The Borghese Gardens,' he yelled to the driver.

'Is that man over there angry with me?' Julie asked, pointing back the way they'd come.

'Oh, no, he's not angry,' Rico said sarcastically. 'He's only saying that your mother was a cow and your father an imp from hell, and he's hoping that your children are all born cross-eyed and with one leg.'

'He doesn't like me much, does he?' Julie asked sunnily.

'What the devil were you thinking of, dashing out into traffic like that?' Rico spoke roughly because he'd had the fright of his life. 'Don't you know about Roman traffic? It doesn't stop for you.'

'That man stopped.'

'And now he can't start again. You'll live under his curse for the rest of your life. And mine, for giving me a heart attack. And what's so damned funny!'

'I'm sorry,' she said, controlling herself and speaking penitently. 'I don't know what's come over me today. I'm just in a holiday mood.'

Rico felt his heart turn over at the sight of her mischievous face. Since she'd arrived in Rome, it was the first time he'd seen her look so merry. Once, happiness had come to her naturally.

He took her hand firmly in his. 'From now on, you stay with me and you don't move,' he commanded.

'*Sì, signore*,' she answered meekly.

Finding the same *carrozza* had been like an omen. What had gone wrong before could be put right this time. The notion was irrational, but who cared about that?

As they clip-clopped along the Via Veneto, Julie became gloriously aware how bright the sun was, how brilliant the colours around her were, how fresh the air, how gentle and attentive her lover was being. She turned on him a smile of such happiness that his own heart was eased, and he managed a smile in return.

She had just terrified him and he was still shaking, but suddenly he, too, saw the sun.

The Borghese Gardens were a paradise of flowers and mysterious paths leading to small temples. As they drove through it, he pointed out its delights to her, venturing to take her hand. But almost at once he had to relinquish it because they had reached the *Giardino Zoologico*.

It was a small, charming zoo. The larger animals were separated from spectators by deep moats rather than cages and given a good deal of carefully designed freedom. Julie eyed the lions, who eyed her scornfully back. She set herself to outstare them and became so preoccupied that she missed the moment Rico slipped away.

He was back in a few minutes, loaded down with ice-cream cones. 'Chocolate,' he said, handing her one, 'because it's your favourite. Mint because it's your second favourite. And pistachio because you haven't tried it before.'

'How do you know I haven't?' she asked, tucking in.

'Whatever you've been doing the past few years, you haven't been in a place where they've made ice cream like this.'

'That's true.'

Keeping the fourth cone for himself, he twined his fingers in hers, and they strolled along together.

'What have you been doing all these years?' he asked casually. 'I know you've become a star, but what else?'

'Very little else,' she said, speaking carefully. Every word had to be examined in case she revealed her secret.

She didn't know that her sudden wariness had sent a shadow flickering across her face. It was gone in an instant, but not before Rico noticed it and wondered.

'You're surely not without friends,' he said a mite too casually. 'There must be someone at home who waits to hear from you. You can't always be calling your friend—what was his name?—Gary?'

'I call lots of people,' she said with a shrug. 'This is really delicious. What's yours like?'

'Delicious,' he said, accepting her change of subject.

It was disconcerting to find that he had to follow her lead. In the days of their first love, she had fallen easily into his arms, never giving him a moment's doubt, never forcing him to court her.

In fact, he'd never courted any woman. In Italy, women queued up to spend an hour on his arm and in his bed. He'd accepted them for what they were, treated them generously and forgotten them.

But now he was being forced to do what other men did—tread softly for fear of driving the beloved woman away. And he found himself in a new country without signposts.

'Why did it have to be that *carrozza*?' he asked.

'It was an omen. Like a second chance.'

He nodded, understanding at once what he would have struggled with before.

They strolled for a couple of hours, hand in hand like children, saying little but enjoying peace and contentment. Then somebody recognized them and a murmur went round. Soon they were being watched everywhere.

Near the elephant house, they found a café and settled outside on wooden chairs to eat snacks. A posse of paparazzi had caught up with them and were clicking determinedly away, rejoicing in the kind of shots nobody had ever thought to see: Rico Forza in casuals, eating burgers and exchanging silly jokes with a woman who made his eyes shine.

'Haven't they got enough by now?' he grunted.

'Oh, let them.' Julie said easily. 'Think how good this is for my career.' She chuckled to herself. 'And think how mad it'll make Mariella.'

'You've really got your knife into her, haven't you?'

'Yes,' Julie said simply.

He grinned. She'd made his day.

When they left the café the press followed them for a while, varying the shots as much as possible, but finally they gave up.

Julie never wanted the day to end. It was a perfect holiday from all the troubles that would still be waiting for her when it was over. But somehow the light was changing, and the troubles would never look quite as bad again. She might even find a way round them.

They chatted about this and that, keeping off dangerous subjects, but growing more at ease with each other until at last no subject seemed impossibly dangerous. Rico ventured to say, 'You once told me that singing made you more alive than anything else—except love.'

'No, that was someone else. That was Patsy Brown.'

'What became of her, Julie?'

'She found it too hard to exist. So now she doesn't. That's all.'

'That's all,' he echoed thoughtfully. 'Who would have thought so much could be contained in just two words?'

'In another time, you told me that you loved me,' she said wistfully. 'Only three words, but the whole world was there. All the world I wanted anyway.'

'Not quite all,' he reminded her. 'You wanted fame, as well.'

'Yes, but not...' She hesitated.

'What?'

'Not at such a price.'

They regarded each other and the truth that lay between them.

'Perhaps the past is too powerful,' she said.

'It doesn't have to be. We can make our own fate.'

She smiled ruefully. 'Spoken like a true Forza. But we can't all be ''rulers of the world''.'

'I don't feel like a ruler of the world,' he confessed. 'I feel like the boy who made you cry and tore his hair because he'd ruined everything.'

'You never made me cry in those days.'

'But I did, once. I was in a bad mood and it made me unkind to you.'

'I can't remember,' she said in a wondering voice.

'I can't forget. I was careful never to be unkind again. It destroyed me to hurt you.'

Silence. What was there to say?

'Mama! Mama!'

They both turned to where a little boy was dancing about in front of the chimpanzees, clutching his father's hand and trying to attract his mother's attention. A short distance away, a young woman was buying ice creams, but she hurried back to her family and let the child point out the animals to her. The father watched them both with a grin of possessive delight.

The boy must have been about the same age as their own son. Julie guessed what Rico was thinking and waited for him to remind her of what they'd lost. She saw his face take on a look of inexpressible sadness, as though a great burden weighed him down. But he said nothing.

After a moment, he gave her hand a squeeze and drew her away. 'Where shall we go now?' he asked.

'I must go back and get ready for tonight's performance.'

He seemed to come out of a dream. 'I'd forgotten about that. I'd forgotten everything.'

'It's been a lovely day, Rico, but the real world is still there.'

'Tomorrow—'

'I can't see you tomorrow,' she said. She'd promised Gary that she wouldn't miss another day.

He frowned. 'Do your plans matter more than being with me?'

She thought of seeing her child again and instinctively smiled. That smile troubled him. It was like the one she'd worn when he'd found her telephoning somebody in the garden of his villa.

'I'm busy tomorrow,' she said lightly but firmly.

'And you won't tell me what?'

'There's a way you could always find out.'

'No,' he said immediately. 'I promised never to have you watched again, and I'm a man of my word.'

'I know you are, Rico. Your word means I'm quite safe.'

'That's a strange thing to say.'

She took his hand. 'Come on. Let's start drifting back.'

They walked slowly for neither really wanted the day to end. By the elephant house, they stood and regarded two huge beasts who were nudging each other fondly with their heads and twining their trunks. Suddenly she laughed softly and pulled him into the shadows.

'If I were an elephant, would you curl your trunk around mine?' she teased.

'Anything that made you happy,' he promised.

That struck her as irresistibly funny and she laughed until she choked. He held on to her, feeling her laughter vibrate through him until he joined in helplessly.

All round, people were heading for the exit as the zoo prepared to close. The eager child was still chattering about everything he saw. Drinks sellers packed up, monkeys scratched and yawned.

In the shadow of the elephant house, a boy and girl kissed.

She found her dressing-room filled with roses, deep red ones from Rico and pink from Beppe. Just as the performance was about to start, the little man put his head round her door.

'We do duets, *sì*?' he asked cheekily.

'We do duets, *sì*,' Julie said.

The little man blew her a kiss and departed, almost colliding with Rico in the doorway. Beppe backed away, kissed both hands at her in a parody of adoration that made Rico pull a face.

'Do women really like that?' he demanded.

'He's fun,' Julie said. 'I like him. We're going to sing together.'

'I'd rather you—that is, is it a good idea?'

'It's a wonderful idea. I like to vary my act.'

'Did you have a pleasant day?' he asked with an effort.

'Yes, I had a lovely time.' She glowed as the memories came rushing back to her.'

'I'm glad.' His smile was a little forced.

He didn't see the smile on Julie's face as he left. It was full of tenderness. She knew what that concession had cost him. What was happening was too wonderful for words. If only it could last.

She spent the next morning rehearsing duets with Beppe. They went well together, and Carlo was thrilled with the result.

Afterwards, as she went to her dressing-room, she heard Rico's voice coming from behind the door of his office, which was slightly open. She hurried past, not wanting to eavesdrop. Even so, she couldn't help hearing, *'Carissima.'*

Darling! Rico was calling somebody 'darling'.

And then he laughed.

That laugh made her feet slow until they stopped altogether. It was tender and affectionate. He'd laughed like that with her at the zoo. And for who else? He laughed again, and the gentle intimacy told her, beyond doubt, that he was talking to a woman.

She gasped and steadied herself against the wall. It couldn't be happening. After yesterday, after the magic time they'd spent together...

She couldn't stop shaking.

It wasn't Mariella on the other end of that phone. Instinct told her that he didn't laugh with the glossy starlet in that fond way. It was a woman who was very dear to him. A woman he'd told her nothing about.

She clenched her hands, taking deep breaths to steady herself.

Then she heard Rico again, speaking softly and with love. 'Anna, *carissima*...'

Now she knew. His beloved was called Anna. Not Julie.

'I have to be going, Anna. I'll come to see you as soon as I can. I'd like to be there for the festival, and we can dance together in the street as we've always done. Goodbye. Take care of yourself.'

Julie moved quickly, closing the door of her dressing-room just as Rico emerged into the corridor. She heard his footsteps growing fainter.

How could this be happening? Rico had turned back to her with love in his eyes, and all the time his real love was elsewhere. It had been another of his tricks.

Something snapped within her. Whatever happened, she had to find Anna, see her, talk to her. There was a simple way of doing that, but strictly speaking, she ought not. Torn by temptation, Julie stayed motionless until she couldn't stand it any longer.

The corridor was empty. It took a moment to slip into Rico's office, lift the phone and touch the redial button.

After two rings, a voice answered, 'Ristorante Tornese.'

She made a hurried excuse and hung up.

She slipped away before Rico could return, then hurried back to the hotel. In her room, she leafed through the telephone directory until she found the Ristorante Tornese in the Piazza Santa Maria in Trastevere.

Now she remembered Rico telling her about Trastevere, the cheerful bohemian quarter that was to Rome what Soho was to London and Greenwich Village to New York. He'd made it sound like a place of colourful life and joy.

And now that was where his heart was.

The next day, she drove out to Fregene to spend another day with Gary. She stayed until he was asleep, then returned to Rome, thoughtful all the way.

It was the policy of La Dolce Notte to feature its star for only six nights of the week. Tuesdays were given over to rising young performers. Today was Tuesday, and Julie was free.

All the way to Rome, she told herself that she wasn't sure what she was going to do tonight. She even returned the car and went back to the hotel thinking that perhaps Rico had left a message for her. He knew it was her free night and would want her to spend it with him.

But there was no message from him, and after sitting in her room for an hour, she called a taxi.

The way to Trastevere lay past the Trevi Fountain and across the River Tiber. Almost as soon as she was on the other side, Julie became aware of a difference in the atmosphere. From somewhere up ahead, she could hear music interspersed by laughing and cheering.

'Here we are,' the driver called cheerfully over his shoulder. 'Just down there is the Piazza Santa Maria in Trastevere. I can't take you any closer because no traffic is allowed.'

The people here seemed to live their lives out on the cobbled streets. High overhead, washing stretched from window to window. Here and there were bars, cafés, their tables spilling out of cramped interiors, sprawling over the pavement. Light poured from every door and window, and from every direction came the sounds of merrymaking.

'My goodness!' she murmured.

The driver grinned. 'It's the festival tonight. Usually it's a little bit quieter. Not much, though.'

She paid him and began to make her way through the crowds. A group of tumblers came streaming along the street. One of them caught her in his arms, swung her round and was gone before she could catch her breath.

In the distance, she could see a hugely tall man walking on stilts. Behind his long legs bounded fire-eaters and dancers in old-fashioned costumes. They might be characters escaped from some Victorian circus, but in these old streets they looked just right.

She found the Ristorante Tornese on a corner. It was a small place but bright and cheerful. All the outside tables were taken and only one remained empty inside. Julie slipped in and took it.

She studied the waitresses and immediately saw the one who must be Anna. She was young and beautiful, with a fresh, angelic quality that made Julie's heart sink.

'What can I get you?' The girl stopped beside her.

'A—a glass of wine, please,' Julie stammered.

'You are ill, *signorina*?' the girl asked anxiously.

Julie pulled herself together. 'No, I'm fine. Just a glass of wine.'

The girl went to fetch it. Julie was close to the kitchen door, which swung back and forth constantly as busy serving staff barged in and out. A large, elderly woman was at the stove, cooking vigorously, surrounded by clouds of steam. She was shabbily dressed in black, with a black kerchief tied about her grey hair.

The door swung to, hiding her from sight, but she appeared a moment later with Julie's wine. 'You all right?' she demanded. 'Sara was worried.'

'Sara? That girl is called Sara? Not Anna?'

'Anna? No.' The old woman gave a bawling laugh. It was rich and earthy, and it shook her huge frame. She laughed and laughed, then wiped her glistening forehead with her black apron. 'I am Anna,' she said.

CHAPTER ELEVEN

'YOU are Anna?' Julie echoed, hardly daring to believe it. 'But you—'

Suddenly Anna let out a yelp of triumph. 'I know you,' she cried. 'You sing at my Rico's place. I see your picture.'

'Yes, I sing at La Dolce Notte. I'm Julie Hallam. And you—you are Rico's Anna?'

The old woman's eyes glowed. 'Rico has told you about me, *sì*?'

'I...well...' She could hardly say that she'd overheard his conversation.

Luckily Anna ploughed on without waiting for an answer. 'Sometimes he calls me Anna. Sometimes Nonna.'

'You are Nonna?' Julie gasped as it all fell into place. 'Yes...I understand now. He told me that he calls you Nonna because you gave him all the love he ever knew.'

'That's my Rico.'

'Anna!' A heavy, middle-aged man had put his head round the kitchen door and bawled at her.

'I return. *Scusi*.' Anna fled into the kitchen.

Through the swinging door, Julie could see the old woman mopping her brow. Another man, out of sight, shouted, 'Anna!' She turned to him and the door swung to, hiding her.

A waiter near Julie hurriedly finished serving and hurtled back into the kitchen, yelling, 'Anna!'

Julie's relief at discovering Anna's identity was replaced by horror. So that weary, overworked woman was the person he claimed to love like a grandmother. He spoke lyrically about what she had done for him, yet here she was, so poor that she had to work like a slave at an age when she ought to be comfortably retired.

She'd loved Rico once for his warm heart. She realized that he'd changed, but had he really changed that much?

The door swung again. This time it was Anna, bearing dishes. As well as cooking, it seemed that she also waited at table. She served some customers near Julie, exchanged backchat with them and returned to Julie, sinking her vast bulk into the chair with a sigh of relief.

'So, my Rico tells you about me,' she continued. 'Always he says nice things about me.'

But he doesn't do nice things for you, Julie thought crossly. Anna's heartfelt joy at the sound of his name was making her angrier with Rico with every passing minute.

'What are you doing in here?' Anna demanded. 'Rico's friend has the best table.'

'It was the only one free—'

'You sit outside where it's nicer.'

She gabbled something in Romagnolo to a boy who looked about sixteen. He scuttled away and returned with a small table that he set up outside with two chairs. Anna whisked a cloth onto it, produced a bottle and two glasses, then indicated for Julie to sit.

'You drink this,' she said, pouring the Chianti. 'Best there is.' She seated herself in the other chair.

'I don't want to get you into any trouble,' Julie said

with a nervous glance at the big man with a moustache who was scowling at Anna.

'Trouble? Hah!' Anna's booming laugh echoed off the walls. 'I been working hard. I wanna sit down, I sit down. What you have to eat?'

'Well—'

'There's some spaghetti carbonara—very nice,' Anna said without letting her speak. 'I get it for you myself.'

She hauled herself to her feet and stomped away. Julie was left feeling as if she'd been flattened by an amiable steamroller.

In no time at all, Anna was back with the spaghetti. She set it down before her, then presented her with a snowy napkin. 'Eat,' she commanded.

'It's delicious,' Julie said after the first mouthful. 'Did you make it?'

'*Sì*. I make everything that is eaten here.'

'Everything?' Julie echoed, aghast. 'But the work must be enormous.'

Anna shrugged. 'I got a boy to help me, but he's an idiot. I tell him get outta my way.'

'You taught Rico to cook, didn't you?'

Anna beamed. 'He tell you that? When?'

Too late, Julie realized that she couldn't answer this without saying more than she wanted. 'Well…' she faltered, 'he's told me a lot about you, how the kitchen was his favourite place because you were there.'

To her relief, Anna allowed herself to be distracted. 'First thing when he gets home from school, always he comes to see me. Who else can he talk to?'

'What about his parents?'

'They are dead before he is ten years old. He lives with his grandfather. I tell you, that old man was a devil. Rico's father, Santo, was his only son. He plans a great marriage for him, but Santo runs away and marries the girl he loves. Maria is a nice, decent girl, but not important enough for Arturo.

'He is very cross, but what can he do? Nothing. The marriage is made and she is pregnant. Then soon after Rico is born, Santo dies. Arturo goes to Maria, and he acts so nice, so gentle, and he says, "Come and live with me."'

'She thinks he is being kind, but that devil only does things for himself. When they are in his house, he pushes her away. He hires a nanny for the baby. Maria hardly ever sees him. Once I hear him tell her, "You are not good enough to be the mother of my grand-son." Can you imagine such wickedness?'

'Yes,' Julie said thoughtfully, 'I can.'

In the light of her own experience, the whole story was horribly believable.

'Didn't she fight for her son?' she asked.

'Nobody could fight him,' Anna said sadly. 'Rico grew up hardly knowing his mother, and at last she gave up fighting. She began to drink too much, and Arturo made sure that there was always drink around. And she loved skiing, so he sent her on long skiing holidays.

'She died in a skiing accident. Perhaps she'd had too much to drink, I don't know. I say Arturo killed her.'

Shocked, Julie was silent. How could the old man have so brutally ignored the needs of the little boy in his obsession to have his own way? And now, of course, his behaviour to her was explained. His son had slipped through his fingers, and it must have seemed that his grandson would do the same. So he'd smashed whoever was in his path to prevent it.

'Arturo told Rico that his mother didn't care for him,' Anna resumed. 'As he grew older, I tried to make him see what had really happened, and now I think he does justice to Maria's memory. But it's not the same as having her when he needed her.'

'No, of course not. But at least he had you.'

Anna smiled fondly. 'He used to cling to me and say, "Nonna, do you love me? Promise that you love me." Such a sad, beautiful little boy. Wait here. I show you something.'

She waddled back into the kitchen but returned at once, carrying a small leather photo album with a worn, well-thumbed look. Anna handed it to Julie. She opened it, and her heart nearly stopped.

Gary's face looked out at her.

'Rico was seven years old there,' Anna said, pointing. 'I took that picture. He had to show me how to work his camera, and I kept pressing the wrong buttons. We laughed so much.'

'He—he was delightful,' Julie stammered.

She'd known Gary was like his father, but seeing Rico at Gary's age showed her how close the likeness was. How they would have loved each other! How much they'd both missed!

Anna's shrewd eyes were on her. Hastily Julie began to leaf through the other pictures: Rico in his early teens, his late teens, and then one that almost made her cry out. There was the boy she'd loved—twenty-three, eager for life, for love. And it had betrayed him.

'Oh, yes,' she whispered to herself. 'That was how he smiled.'

Anna didn't answer, but her eyes saw everything.

There was only one more picture, obviously taken recently. This was Rico as she'd seen him when she first arrived—stern, unsmiling.

'I used to hope he'd find some girl who'd love him truly and make him happy,' Anna sighed.

'And—and did he ever find her?' Julie asked, concentrating on her food.

'Once…long ago. He thought she was an angel. When he told me about her, his face shone with joy. He couldn't stop talking about her, how perfect she was, how she was going to have his baby. He'd known so little love and he was so grateful to her for loving him. Once he said to me, "I would lay down my life for her." But…' Anna shrugged sadly. 'She abandoned him. Since then, he's never been the same. His heart withered. That is what she did to him.'

The bright good humour had faded from the old woman's face, leaving behind the unforgiving judgement of a mother figure for someone who had wounded her young.

'But perhaps it wasn't her fault,' Julie urged. 'Don't forget what you know about Arturo. Maybe he forced her to abandon him.'

Anna shrugged. '*Sì*. It would be like him. But she gave away Rico's child. How can she have loved him and do that? I tell you, that was when he knew that her love was a sham. And if such a thing could happen with her, then every woman's love was a sham.

'I don't know all that happened. Even with me, there is much he keeps to himself. But I know this. He was once a boy with a warm, loving heart. He became a man who loves nobody.' Her eyes glinted with sudden shrewdness. 'But perhaps you can make him love again.'

'Me...I...' She was dismayed to find herself blushing.

'I see the pictures of you two together in all the papers.'

'Anna, you can't believe what you see in the papers. People like to believe that Rico and I—I mean, it's good for business.'

'Business! Hah!' Anna snorted. 'And what about you? You don't love him?'

'I...' Julie floundered. But the next moment, Anna came to her rescue.

'*Idiota*!' she said, striking herself on the forehead. 'Where are my manners to ask you such a thing? Mind your own business, Anna. You are *cretina*!'

Julie dissolved into laughter, relieved to have been let off the hook. 'I don't think you are,' she said. 'But I can't talk about him—not just now.'

'Of course. And your plate is empty. I bring more food.

'No, please...'

But she was talking to empty air. Anna had vanished into the kitchen, bawling instructions as she went.

Julie was glad of the respite. It was true that she couldn't speak openly about Rico, but neither could she dissimulate with this earthy, honest woman. Although they'd only met a short time ago, she already knew that Anna's shrewd eyes would see through any pretence.

Obviously she didn't know the truth. If she did, she would judge Julie harshly. And Julie instinctively cared about her opinion.

Anna came roaring back with a plate piled high,

which she set down in front of Julie. 'Eat, eat, eat!' she commanded. 'You are too thin.'

'I need to be thin,' she protested. 'I have to wear glamorous dresses that show every extra ounce. If I can't get into them, I shall tell Rico it's your fault.'

Anna screamed with laughter. It was so infectious that Julie joined in, which made Anna laugh even more. She reached out and took Julie's face between her hands. They were warm, steady hands and they gave her a strange jolt of happiness. She, too, had lacked the steady love of a mother and she suddenly understood exactly why Anna was so important to Rico.

Then Anna's face brightened still more. A look of utter delight swept over it, and the next moment she'd bounded out of her seat, arms flung wide in ecstatic greeting. 'Rico!'

Julie looked round to find the two of them locked in a fierce embrace. Rico hugged Anna robustly, then looked into her face. His own face was transformed. All the cynical sophistication that marred it had vanished, to be replaced by heartfelt joy.

'I was afraid you don't come,' Anna told him at the top of her voice.

'You know I can't stay away from you,' he said with a grin.

'See who's here.' Anna nodded towards Julie.

Julie wondered if he would be annoyed at finding her here, but Rico said mildly, 'Yes, I saw. You two seem to be getting on well.'

'She's a nice girl,' Anna hissed. 'You sit down with her while I get food.'

She bustled away. A waiter indicated that he was

ready to take his order, but Rico waved him away. 'Anna will serve me,' he said.

From deep in the kitchen, they could hear Anna making her presence felt to the accompaniment of crashing plates.

'She's certainly putting herself out to please you,' Julie observed.

'She always does. She likes it.'

'But how old is she?'

'I don't know. Probably over sixty.'

'Over sixty? And what time will she finish working here?'

Rico stared at her. 'What are you saying?'

'She won't finish until after midnight, will she?'

'Much later. The festival is on.'

His calm tone galled her and she snapped, 'I expect she started at midday?'

'Earlier, probably. She buys food in the market first.'

'You have the nerve to say that you love her and yet you let her live like this?' Julie said indignantly. 'She's an old woman. She ought to be putting her feet up, not working herself to death because you're too mean to give her a decent pension.'

He looked at her curiously. 'I see. So that's what you're mad about.'

'I'll say I am. If you could hear the way she talks about you. Everything is "my Rico". She thinks you're wonderful. Why are you staring at me?'

'I—was I?'

'You looked as if you'd seen a ghost. Never mind that. Let's talk about Anna and the way you're treating her.'

For the next few minutes, her words washed over

him. His mind was filled with pictures of Miko the horse, the nameless dog in the pub, and a young girl who only ever became angry when she was defending the vulnerable. The memories made a spring of happiness well up in him.

Over her shoulder, he saw Anna bearing down on them, armed with laden plates. He leaned back out of Julie's line of sight and gave Anna a huge wink before barking out, 'Hurry up. I'm hungry.'

Julie stared, outraged at his tone.

'*Scusi, scusi,*' Anna mumbled, hurriedly setting down the plates before them.

'I should think so,' Rico said curtly. 'And get some salt, fast. There's none on this table.'

'I've been in such a hurry,' Anna said humbly.

'Always excuses,' Rico sneered. 'If it happens again, I'll complain to your employer. *Hey!*'

The shout was the result of having a plate of spaghetti tossed over him. Julie rose to her feet, eyes flashing. 'You ought to be ashamed of yourself,' she seethed. 'How dare you talk to Anna like that after all she's done for you! It's bad enough that you let her slave here till all hours at everyone's beck and call—what's so funny?'

Rico and Anna had collapsed with laughter. They clung together and rocked back and forth, helpless with mirth. Julie sat down and looked uncertainly from one to the other.

'You bad boy!' Anna chided him, starting to clean him up. 'Why do you make fun of this nice girl?' She patted Julie's hand. 'This restaurant is mine.'

'Yours?'

'My Rico has bought it for me. Also two others.'

'Oh,' Julie said in a hollow voice.

'I bought them as an investment so that Anna could retire on the proceeds,' Rico said. 'I meant her to take it easy, but she won't.'

'I like to cook and be with people,' Anna said. 'Who wants to put their feet up and be alone?'

'But everyone was yelling at you,' Julie protested.

Anna shrugged. 'So? That idiot over there is my brother. The two younger idiots are his sons. They yell at me, I yell at them. So what?'

Right on cue, an unseen presence inside bawled, 'Anna!'

'I go,' she declared, heaving her bulk up from the chair and waddling away.

'I must go and get cleaned up,' Rico said. He laid a hand on her arm. 'You won't leave?'

'No.'

'Promise,' he said urgently.

'I promise.'

He was gone barely five minutes, and when he returned he was wearing a clean white shirt. 'I keep a room and some clothes here,' he explained.

'Then this is your real home? Not the villa.'

'I suppose that's true. Yes, it is true. I come here when I want to be made a fuss of.'

'What a fool I was,' Julie said sheepishly. 'I should have known you wouldn't keep her slaving away.'

'How should you know? It's my fault if you think the worst of me. But I'm so glad you two like each other.'

'I think she's wonderful.'

'What made you come here?'

'I was eavesdropping when you were on the phone to her, and I was curious.'

'Curious? Does that mean jealous?'

She considered. 'Yes,' she said at last. 'It does.'

'I'm glad. I should hate to think all the jealousy was on my side.' He looked at her with meaning.

'Beppe?' she asked hilariously.

'Don't be fooled by his age or his waistline. Women fall for him in droves.'

'And I understand why.'

'Oh, you do?'

'I love his sense of humour.'

'I never had very much of that,' he said wryly.

'No.' She smiled. 'But you had a lot of other things that I remember very well.'

'Were you really jealous of Anna?'

'You'll never know how much.'

She had to raise her voice to be heard over the sound of a trombone. A band was passing along the street, making unskilled but vigorous noises.

'It's Noiantri,' Rico shouted.

'What is?' she shouted back.

When the band had gone by, he said, 'In Trastevere, we celebrate the festival of Noiantri every year. The word means. "We Others" in Romagnolo, the Roman dialect. That's how we think of ourselves here. We're different. We believe that we're the only true descendants of the ancient Romans.'

'We? You talk as though you were one of them.'

'I feel like one of them. Like you said, this is my real home.'

All around them, couples were dancing in the piazza while fireworks whizzed and roared overhead. Rico held out his hand and swept her away into the noisy, jostling crowd.

They danced any old way, bouncing here and there, clinging to each other and laughing joyously. A man stood up to sing in a hoarse, unpolished voice, and everyone cheered him wildly. The band blared. Rico swung her round and round until she was giddy, and then there were only his lips on hers.

'Come with me,' he whispered.

'Yes, anywhere.'

Together they climbed the narrow stairs to the little room in the apartment over the café. Plainly furnished, it held only a wardrobe and a bed just big enough for lovers.

At first they just stood in silence their arms around each other, feeling at last a deep peace in each other's presence.

'Are you really here?' he whispered.

'Yes, my darling, I'm here…I'm here.'

'And you won't go away again?'

She couldn't answer because his mouth had already covered hers, his lips caressing her gently, eagerly. He kissed her mouth, her eyes, her forehead, touching her with reverence.

When they were undressed and lying on the bed, he didn't try to claim her at once, but held her body against the length of his own. The passion was growing between them, but tonight, something was even more important. They had come home to each other's arms.

They lay together, watching the sky light up as fireworks streaked up into the sky and fell in glittering showers. Their eyes met, and they shared a smile full of mystery and understanding. Rico began to kiss her gently and caress her body with tender, loving movements. The old joy came flooding back. Julie felt her heart flower again as her body responded to his desire with an ardour of its own.

She had been made for him, and him only. She returned his kisses, delighted at his instant reaction.

'You're beautiful,' he murmured. 'How have I lived so long without you?'

She couldn't speak. His skilful hands were moving over her, escalating desire wherever they lingered. She wanted him so much, and the feel of his face between her breasts was inexpressibly sweet.

He loved her gently, as though he feared that she might break in his arms. And she felt safe with him, as she had thought never to feel again. It was wonderful to be able to shower her gifts on him again and sense the passionate gratitude in his response.

That gratitude had always been there, she recognized. As a boy, his loneliness had made him imbue her every caress with significance so that he had almost worshipped her when she'd nursed him through a minor illness.

The lonely boy had grown into a lonely man who needed her love now more than ever. And she had grown into a woman of depth and profound tenderness, who could instil in him desire, but also something else, infinitely more precious.

She showed him in actions, enfolding him in her arms in a gesture of protection, silently promising to keep him enclosed for ever in the haven of her love.

It was he who slept first and she who lay awake, watching over him, keeping vigil against the world.

CHAPTER TWELVE

THEY slept with their arms around each other. Julie awoke feeling relaxed and happy. Rico was just opening his eyes and stretching like a contented cat. She kissed him, slipped out of the narrow bed and went to the window.

Outside, the street lights were beginning to fade, as the first gleam of dawn appeared. As the doors closed on the last of the night's revellers, the early stallholders were throwing open their windows, yawning and rubbing their eyes.

'Doesn't this place ever go completely to sleep?' Julie asked contentedly.

'Never quite,' Rico replied, coming close and slipping his arms around her from behind. 'There's always some activity or other going on.'

'I used to dream of this,' she murmured, leaning back against him. 'Long ago, when you first told me about Trastevere and I saw us living here, I thought of it just like this. It was such a lovely dream.'

'Is it a lovely dream to be poor?'

'I've always been poor. The thought didn't scare me. And I had you—or thought I had. That was riches enough.'

'You had me,' he assured her. 'You never knew how much I loved you. I couldn't find the words to tell you. I tried, but what came out was a pale shadow of the truth.'

She knew what he meant. It had been the same with

her. She'd offered him heartfelt words, but they hadn't seemed enough. She consoled herself with the thought that she would give him a baby and show her feelings in actions.

But she couldn't tell him this now. So she remained silent, only turning her head to feel his lips on her forehead.

'It was a dream,' she mused. 'People aren't allowed to be as happy as we were, or not for long. One brief glimpse of heaven, just enough to torment you all your life. Perhaps it would be better not to see heaven at all.'

'Hush, you don't really believe that.'

'No, I don't believe it. I can never forget what we had or how beautiful it was. We'll always have those memories.'

'You speak as if everything was over for us, as though there could never be any future. But there has to be. We can't lose each other again.

'I want to tell you something. I realize now that I was wrong to blame you. It took me too long to face that it was my fault. I should have told you the truth about myself all those years ago. At first it was a game, pretending to be poor and knowing that you loved me as a poor man, for myself alone. I almost worshipped you for that.

'I pictured myself returning from Italy, telling you the truth, showering you with luxuries. But I never though of what I'd done to you—leaving you vulnerable. It's true I didn't dream what my grandfather would do, but that's no excuse. I knew him. I should have thought. But I didn't, and when the crisis came, you were defenceless. How could I do that to you?

And how could I blame you afterwards when I'd left you to face it alone?'

He took her face between his hands. 'Do you understand? I blame you for nothing, nothing. The blame is all mine.'

It was the declaration of perfect love and trust that she had longed for. He was Rico again, as she'd always longed to find him. And now, at last, it was safe to tell him everything.

'Rico, there's something—'

Her words were cut off by a knock on the door, and Anna's voice saying urgently, 'Rico, Rico!'

'What is it, Nonna,' he called back.

'There's a phone call from Milan. Quickly.'

'They call you here?' Julie asked.

'Only if it's something very urgent,' he said. 'Damn. I'm coming, Nonna.'

He pulled on his clothes in a hurry and the next moment he was gone.

She could have cried out at the ruin of her perfect moment. But underlying dismay, there was still happiness. What had just happened between them could never be taken away. The moment would come again.

She dressed and went along to the little kitchen. Anna, vast and impressive in dressing-gown and curlers, was at the stove. She grinned at Julie, thrust a coffee into her hand and pointed to the next room from where they could hear Rico's voice.

Julie took him the coffee. He was talking in angry, urgent tones.

'We had an agreement...he can't go back on it now...tell them to do nothing until I get there...yes, I'll be there today.'

He hung up, drank his coffee and gave her a brief kiss.

'Will you be away long?' she asked.

'A few days. There's a meeting I must get to.' He touched her face gently. 'Why did it have to happen now, when we have found each other again?'

'When you return—'

'Yes, it will be soon. Suddenly his face darkened and he held her tightly. 'Will you be here? Shall I return to find you gone again?'

'Never, my love.'

'Promise me.'

'I promise. Rico, don't be afraid. Things are different now.'

'For years I had this nightmare. Always in dreams, I returned home calling your name, and you were never there. Don't let me fall into that nightmare again.'

'The nightmare is over,' she vowed. 'Trust me, Rico. Can't you trust me?'

'Yes,' he said with a slight effort. 'Of course I trust you. What were you going to say before Nonna called me?'

'It can wait until you get back.'

'I'll call you.'

'Use this number,' she said, scribbling her mobile number. 'Then you'll find me anywhere. Goodbye, my love. Come back to me.'

Strangely enough, his absence was one of the happiest times Julie had ever known. She visited Gary daily, performed to rapturous audiences and dreamed about the future.

She visited Anna, who asked no questions but seemed to understand without words. She even let Julie into Rico's room where she could sit and feel his presence. That was how she discovered that he had kept the note she'd written him long ago. Its brutality distressed her and she crumpled it up, praying for the chance to make it up to him for all he'd suffered.

Rico returned from Milan in a glad state of mind. He'd taken care of his enemies, imposed his authority and was eagerly anticipating a reunion with the woman he loved. He planned to call Julie as soon as he reached the villa.

But a surprise awaited him at his home. A stream of servants ferrying suitcases packed to bulging came down the stairs and out to a waiting van. His steward informed him that Mariella had been there for the past hour. He found her in the room that had been hers. Wardrobe doors stood open, revealing that nothing was left inside. Drawers were empty. The room had been stripped as bare as if a plague of locusts had swarm over it.

It was the first time they'd seen each other since the night at the club when he'd floored Barono.

'I came for my things,' she said. 'Salvatore has implored me to leave you and live with him. He says I deserve a man who understands women.'

'I hope you haven't left anything behind,' Rico said, regarding her looting with tolerant cynicism.

Mariella shrugged. 'If I have, Salvatore will buy whatever I need.'

'I hear you're going to be in his next film. I hope you'll be very happy together.'

'He says I'm the love of his life,' Mariella declaimed in throbbing accents.

'How nice.'

'I have even persuaded him not to sue you for assaulting him.'

'So I expected,' Rico said. 'It would spoil the story if my real reason was aired in court, wouldn't it?' She scowled, and he added hastily, 'But it's very kind of you.'

'Yes, I think it is, too, after the way you treated me.'

'I don't think you did so badly out of me. We were always honest with each other, Mariella. There was no pretence of love on either side.'

'And you think you're going to find love with your stupid English girl?'

'Leave her out of it,' Rico said quietly.

'She's really played you for a sucker. Those demure manners, butter wouldn't melt in her mouth. And all the time she's making a fool of you.'

'*That's enough*!' Rico snapped. 'You know nothing about her.'

'Don't I? Ask her to tell you who Gary is—if you dare.'

Rico's shrug was a masterpiece of indifference. 'Gary is a friend. I know all about him.'

'Do you know how often she visits him when your back is turned?'

Rico turned very pale. 'What the devil are you talking about?'

'He's here in Italy because she couldn't bear to be apart from him. While you were away, she spent every day with him.'

Suddenly the nightmare was there again—the absence, the return to find everything different, love gone, only emptiness left. The details were a little changed, but the pain was the same.

Julie had tried to tell him something before his departure. What was it?

He'd telephoned her. She'd always been there. But that was her mobile phone. She'd made a point of giving him the number. She might have been anywhere.

What had she wanted to tell him?

With a supreme effort, he assumed an air of confidence in front of Mariella. Hell could freeze over before he'd let her suspect his agony.

'You're lying,' he said. 'Don't try to make trouble between Julie and me.'

Mariella gave a catlike smile. 'All right, darling. I'll just leave you to find out for yourself. I hope your disillusion isn't too painful.'

'Hope it is, you mean,' Rico said, eyeing her coldly.

She shrugged. 'Whatever.'

'I've made a mess of everything,' Rico groaned.

'Hah! You only just find that out?' Anna snorted. She slapped down a plate of spaghetti carbonara in front of him. 'Eat!'

'How can I eat when everything is over?'

'Eat. Then it won't be over.'

'Thanks, Nonna.'

'Don't call me Nonna. You think I want anyone knowing I helped raise an idiot?'

Rico managed a faint grin, not at all offended by this blunt talk. If anything, it pleased him, for it brought back the days when he'd sat in the grandiose kitchen at the villa, talking over his troubles with the only person who understood.

The kitchen of Anna's little apartment was far from grandiose, but it had the same smells of garlic, tomatoes and pepper, all of which he associated with comfort. There was comfort, too, in the sound of her bustling about, yelling at him with the disrespect of a grandmother in pungent Romagnolo. He answered in the same dialect.

'It seemed so simple when I planned it,' he mused between mouthfuls. 'But things went wrong from the moment I saw her again.'

'Of course. Things never work out as you plan them.'

'They did for the old man.'

'That's because he had no heart. He was ruthless, so he could forget about people. You're not like that.'

'I'd forgotten how she could affect me—after all those years. I got confused and I made mistakes. That night we went out in the *carrozza*—it seemed such a good idea. Change tactics, romance her until she lost her head and told me what I wanted to know—about my son—because she's the girl who—'

'You think I don't know who she is? I knew from the moment she walked in.'

'Yes, I suppose you did. But I was the one who lost my head. Suddenly it was like being boy and girl again, and I wanted the night to go on forever—just to be with her. I'd forgotten that my spies were watching. And she noticed them—'

Anna said an extremely rude word. Romagnolo has some of the best rude words in the world, and this one cast serious doubt on Rico's paternity, his intelligence and even his sanity. But he seemed to find it fair, for he responded with a wry face.

'She was very angry—'

'*You don't say*!' Anna bawled sarcastically. 'Well, well! She was angry. Fancy that! What was she supposed to do when she discovered her lover was spying on her? Kiss your feet?'

'She wasn't supposed to know. I was going to call them off after that, but she discovered them first and walked out on me. So then I got angry, too, and I made her sing at my home that night—and Mariella was there on my arm—'

'So Julie thought you didn't care about her because you got Mariella? Give me patience!'

'And it got worse, and then...I don't know. Every time I thought I was finding the way—things went wrong.'

'You mean you did something stupid?'

'I did many things that were stupid.'

'But this was ages ago,' Anna said. 'Since then, the two of you came here and you made it up. So she forgave you.'

'I thought she had. Now I'm not so sure. There's this other man. His name is Gary. I've heard her talk to him on the phone with such a note in her voice— the note that used to be there only for me. I thought she loved me, Nonna,' he went on wretchedly. 'But she's been stringing me along—and it's my own fault.'

Anna sighed. 'Oh, Rico! What hope is there for you when you go about with blinkers? She loves you. I could see that at once.'

'Then why isn't she frank with me?'

'Perhaps she's afraid of you. You've become a harsh man who judges easily. But with this woman, you're different. She's your best hope unless you throw her away. Do something quickly.'

'What can I do, Nonna? It's too late. I told you, she's got someone else.'

Anna snorted her contempt for all men. She set coffee before him, then picked up her handbag. After rummaging through it, she took out a piece of paper and gave it to him.

Rico studied it, puzzled. It bore an address in Fregene.

'My niece has a villa at Fregene. She recognized Julie from her picture in the paper and called me to boast about her famous neighbour.'

'Has she seen this man?' Rico asked.

'She has seen Gary. Now stop asking questions and go to Fregene!'

Julie knew that Rico was due home at any moment. He said he'd call her when he arrived, but the hours passed with no word from him.

She finally called the villa and learned from the steward that Rico had arrived back three hours ago but had gone out again at once.

The afternoon wore on into the evening. As always, she put her feet up for an hour in the hotel. But she couldn't doze off. She was waiting for Rico to call. And he didn't.

Then it was time for the evening's performance. He would be there waiting for her. But he wasn't.

She tried to be reasonable. He must have a lot to see to on his return. But the silence was unnerving. It took all her professionalism to give of her best that night. Both her mind and her heart were in turmoil.

She slept badly and awoke to the sound of the phone. It was Cassie, and she sounded agitated. 'I'm sorry to call you so early, but I'm worried. I think we're being watched.'

Instantly Julie sat up straight in bed, every nerve screaming. 'Has anyone approached you?'

'No, but there's this car. I can see it from the window. It was there yesterday. Then it drove away, but last night it came back and it hasn't moved.'

'Lock all the doors,' Julie said urgently. 'Don't answer to anyone except me. I'm on my way.'

She was downstairs in a few minutes and hired one of the hotel cars. Soon she was on the road to Fregene, driving as fast as she dared, her mind seething with questions and fears.

Rico had been watching the house all night. She had no doubt that it was him. Somehow he'd found her hideaway and was waiting his moment to pounce. That was why he hadn't told her he was back. He planned to spirit Gary away while she was unaware. Oh, why had she been so careless as to bring Gary here? How could she stop Rico from snatching him?

She feared the worst as she drew up by the beach at Fregene, but Rico's car was still there. The doors were closed and the windows rolled up, and at first she thought it was empty.

She began to run to the house but stopped when she thought she heard someone call her name. She turned. Rico was getting out of his car.

'Julie...' he said. He sounded hesitant.

'Stay here,' she cried, flinging out a hand to ward him off. She ran towards him, keeping between him and the house. 'Rico, please, listen to me.'

His face was ravaged. 'Will it help—talking? Will it change anything?'

'Nothing can change the past, but if I could make you understand—'

'Why did you lie to me? Why couldn't you have told me the truth all this time?'

She'd come close to him. 'I was afraid of what you'd do.'

'I'd never do anything to hurt you, Julie. I love you too much. When you first came here, I was crazy with pain—I'd have done anything. But it was no good. I still loved you, and it was too much for me. I thought—' he drew a ragged breath '—I thought we'd found each other again.'

'So did I. Rico, I love you.'

'Don't lie to me. Julie, I know. Don't you understand? I know you're in love with another man. I know he's in that house.'

'You know...?' she whispered.

'Everything. You've been visiting him while I was away. I ought to hate you for that, but I can't. I can't hate you for anything. Why did you do it? Was it your idea of revenge? Did I deserve it?'

She searched his face. Some part of the truth was beginning to dawn on her, but it was too wonderful to be easily believed. 'How can you believe such a thing of me?' she breathed.

'I came here yesterday, determined to confront your lover. But I couldn't do it. I sat here for hours, then I drove away again.

'I came back last night, but I still couldn't make myself knock on that door. If I don't see his face, maybe he isn't real.' He gave a mirthless laugh. 'I was afraid. Can you imagine that? I've never been afraid of anything, and yet—'

'Rico—'

'Does he truly love you, Julie? Love you as much as I do? I don't believe it. After all we've meant to each other, can't you forgive me and start again? Does this man—this Gary—really mean so much to you?'

'Yes,' she said steadily. 'Gary means all the world to me. We've loved each other for almost eight years, and I can't do without him.'

Rico's shoulders sagged. 'In that case, there's nothing for me to do but leave.'

'No, I want you to meet him.'

'What would be the use of that? Let it go, Julie. I was wrong. I bear you no ill will. You did what you had to do. But eight years! You turned to him very soon after me, didn't you?'

'A few months,' she said with a little smile. 'Rico, I promise you, when you meet Gary, you will understand everything.'

Something in her voice made him go very quiet. Had the first hint of the truth begun to reach him? Julie took his hand and led him across the sand towards the villa. She opened the front door. On the threshold, Rico paused, still uncertain.

'Gary,' Julie called. 'Come here, my darling.'

He usually came dashing towards her, but today the child seemed to know something was different. He pushed open the kitchen door and stood there, blackhaired, dark-eyed, the image of the man facing him.

Julie put a hand on his shoulder and smiled down at him in reassurance. He returned the smile, and Rico's heart nearly stopped. For in that smile the child was like his mother, too.

'I've brought someone for you to meet,' Julie said.

Man and boy looked at each other in silence. At last, Rico drew a long, slow breath. 'Are you...Gary?'

The child nodded. 'Who are you?'

'I'm...' The words wouldn't come. It had been eight long years. Rico dropped down to one knee in front of his son and looked into the eyes that were so like his own. He tried again. 'I'm your—'

'This is your father,' Julie told the child gently.

Gary's expression became intent. He studied Rico's face, meeting his eyes candidly, unafraid. He was a son any man would be proud of. The sight broke Rico and he reached out blindly, drawing the little boy hard against him and hiding his face. Julie saw his shoulders shaking and covered her eyes, which had blurred suddenly.

'All this time,' Rico said huskily. 'All this time...'

He pulled back and discovered that his son was regarding him curiously. The child put out a tentative hand and touched the tears on his father's face. His Italian side was very strong in him, and even at seven he wasn't afraid of emotion.

'Why are you crying?' he asked.

'Because I'm happy,' Rico managed to say.

'Is that why Mommy's crying, too?'

'I think so—I hope so.'

The little boy looked from one to the other. Julie's heart was overflowing and she was beyond speech. Rico got to his feet.

'Julie,' he whispered, 'why didn't you—'

'I didn't dare tell you. All those years when Arturo was alive, I was afraid for you. But I took his money only to help me raise Gary. Then, when I came here, I was afraid *of* you. I've been waiting, hoping for the moment when I could tell you the truth. How could you believe I would give away our son—all I had left of you?'

'I think in my heart I never could really believe it. That you seemed able to do such a thing left me bewildered. It was so unlike you. And all this time you have been as good and true as I remembered from our happy days. You have been…you.'

He gathered her into his arms, not kissing her, but holding her against his heart, his cheek against her hair, while his tears flowed unrestrained.

There was no need for words in the passing away of all sadness between them. She lifted her head and he looked into her face, clearly seeing the truth and beauty that had always been there if he'd only known how to recognize it.

'Mine,' he said huskily.

'Always yours. My heart is yours, my son is yours, and my life is yours.'

He spoke solemnly. 'I tell you that my heart has never belonged to another woman, no matter what—'

'Hush,' she silenced him. 'We need no explanations. Only the future matters.'

'You'll stay here now, with me. We'll be married.' The words were half a command, half a plea.

'Yes, we'll be married. Gary and I will never leave you again.'

'And we'll be a true family at last. Oh, my dearest…'

His mouth was on hers in the first kiss of their new love. They clung together like castaways who had finally found a safe haven.

A tall, elderly woman had slipped into the room. Gary turned to her, puzzled. 'Aunt Cassie, why are they crying *and* kissing?'

'Let's leave them alone,' she said drawing him away. 'And I'll try to explain.…'

Mother's Day is Around the Corner...
Give the gift that celebrates Life and Love!

Show Mom you care by presenting her with a one-year subscription to:

HARLEQUIN WORLD'S BEST *Romances*

For only $4.96—
That's **75% off the cover price.**

This easy-to-carry, compact magazine delivers 4 exciting romance stories by some of the very best romance authors in the world.

Plus each issue features personal moments with the authors, author biographies, a crossword puzzle and more...

A one-year subscription includes 6 issues full of love, romance and excitement to warm the heart.

To send a gift subscription, write the recipient's name and address on the coupon below, enclose a check for $4.96 and mail it today. In a few weeks, we will send you an acknowledgment letter and a special postcard so you can notify this lucky person that a fabulous gift is on the way!

ℋarlequin Romance®

Coming Next Month

#3599 HONEYMOON HITCH Renee Roszel
Jake has made it clear that he wants children from his marriage of
convenience with Susan. Yet, while Susan yearns for Jake's love
without having experienced a kiss from him, the most daunting thing
on the horizon isn't their wedding day…but their wedding night!
The Merits of Marriage

#3600 HUSBAND ON DEMAND Leigh Michaels
Jake Abbott goes to his brother's house to find peace and quiet in
which to work—only to discover that Cassie has been hired to look
after the residence. He's clearly very happy for their temporary living
arrangements to become more intimate. But what about making them
permanent…?
Hiring Ms. Right

#3601 MATILDA'S WEDDING Betty Neels
Matilda tries to ignore her strong attraction to Dr. Henry Lovell. After
all, he is her boss *and* engaged to someone else! But soon Henry starts
to find Matilda just as intriguing as she finds him….
White Weddings

#3602 A WIFE WORTH KEEPING Rosemary Carter
Samantha had left her husband, Max Anderson, when she thought he'd
been unfaithful. Now, a year later, she's forced to live with him in order
to secure their little daughter's inheritance. But how long can she
resist Max when her feelings for him continue to be so powerful…?